A BLAKE HARTE MYSTERY

REACH

ROBERT INNES

Copyright © 2017 Robert Innes
Cover designed by Ashley Mcloughlin

1st Edition: July 18th 2017

All rights reserved. This book or any portion thereof may not be reproduced or used in any manner whatsoever without the express written permission of the author except for the use of brief quotations in a book review.

All characters appearing in this work are fictitious. Any resemblance to real persons, living or dead is purely coincidental.

For questions and comments about this book, please contact the author at rgwisox@aol.com.

ISBN: 9781521916087
Imprint: Independently Published.

A BLAKE HARTE MYSTERY BOOK 4

ROBERT INNES

OTHER BLAKE HARTE BOOKS

Untouchable
Confessional
Ripples
Reach

CHAPTER
ONE

The loud metallic slam of the steel door reverberated around the confined corridor. Blake waited for the guard to check that it was properly locked before they continued. He glanced up at the other cells. From all angles he could hear the sounds of jeers and shouts from the prisoners around him, but it was a cacophony that did not allow him to distinguish any particular words.

"They can tell there's a copper amongst them," murmured the guard as they began walking along the corridor again. "You're a braver man than me."

Blake gave him the smallest of insincere smiles, but said nothing. His mind was more concerned with who he was here to see. None of the thugs around him came close in their intentions to the man he was about to clap eyes on for the first time in seven years.

As the sound of the other prisoners faded away, the corridor became darker as they made their way further down below the building to the high security wing. Blake's stomach churned uncomfortably as they reached a final large steel door and the guard turned to him.

"I'm sure I don't need to tell you this, DS Harte, but still. Quite why you've agreed to see him, I have no idea, but here we are. There will be someone in the room with you at all times. This is non-negotiable, no matter what either you or he might say, but then he knows that. If you feel uncomfortable at any time, you give the signal and we get you out of there. All clear?"

Blake nodded. "Is he cuffed?"

"He is," replied the guard. "Not that it'll stop his mouth from working, so let me reiterate. If he crosses the line, we will get you out there."

"Good," replied Blake, straightening his shirt and tie, more for something to do with his hands than for appearances sake. "Though, I'll be the one who decides when it's over, thanks. I don't need saving. I was the one who put him here, remember."

"Exactly," the guard said sternly, pulling a bolt

across on the door. "And you're not the only one who knows that. Alright, in you go."

The door squeaked loudly as it opened and Blake stepped inside the room. It was dark and chilly. The walls around him were made of solid grey stone, and a weak flickering optic light in the ceiling was the only thing stopping Blake stepping into complete blackness. In the centre of the otherwise empty room was a large table with two chairs opposite one another. The guard stepped in behind Blake and closed the door behind them and the echo resonated around the room. Blake barely noticed it. He was concentrating on the man sat at the table.

Blake knew that the man was in his fifties, but his appearance gave the impression of somebody much older. His face was sallow and he appeared to be quite frail, but Blake was only too aware of what the man was capable of. Thomas Frost looked up at Blake and smiled.

"Hello, Mr Harte," he whispered, his voice silky and smooth. "It's been a long time."

Blake didn't reply. He merely walked across the room and sat down opposite Frost, crossing his arms, hoping that it was not an action that betrayed his own nervousness.

The flickering light above them slightly illuminated Frost's yellowing teeth and he continued smiling coldly at Blake. "Thank you for coming. I wasn't sure if you would. Or even could."

"Neither was I," replied Blake.

"So, why did you?" Frost asked him, leaning forward slightly. Blake would have liked to be able to see for himself that Frost's hands were cuffed, but he knew he was going to have to take the guard's word for it.

"I was curious," Blake said.

"Perhaps a little *nostalgic*?" Frost murmured. "From what I gather, I was your big break. The case that gave you those letters that you use so proudly before your name. I bet you found it irresistible to come and see me."

"Whatever my reasons, I'm here now," Blake replied. "What do you want?"

Frost's smile faded slightly. Blake could tell he had been eager to toy with him further, but Blake knew that humouring him was something he needed to avoid. "I wanted to take a trip down memory lane with you." He paused, perhaps to give Blake a chance to question him, but when he got no response, he continued. "Cast your mind back seven years. Seven years, six months and nineteen days, to be precise. The day that judge sent me here."

Blake remembered it well. The courtroom had been full, more so than any court Blake had ever stood in, mostly full of media and other policemen Blake had worked with on Frost's case. Just before Frost had been taken away, he had stared straight at Blake; a stare that Blake graphically remembered making his blood run cold.

"The day you were put in here for the rest of your life, and then some," Blake answered. "I remember."

"Remind me."

"Why?"

"Because I want you to."

"Tough."

Frost chuckled. "What's the matter, Mr Harte? Is it the fact that here we are, sat at a table again, having a conversation about everything I did, all those women I killed. And *yet*, now, you don't know what to say. You don't like me being the one with the upper hand?"

Blake rolled his eyes. "I'm clearly wasting my time." He began to stand up. "Unlike you, I have a life to live. And I'm not going to waste it playing riddles with you."

He turned and walked back towards the door. The guard was about to unlock it when Frost stopped him in his tracks. "Kerry Nightingale will be dead by the end of the week."

Blake and the guard exchanged looks.

"The one woman you thought you'd saved. But I promise you, I will see her dead by the end of the week. And there's nothing you'll be able to do to save her. She *will* die. Just like the rest. Just when you think she's at her safest."

Blake bit his lip in regret before turning round. He was breaking his own promise about humouring him, but he needed to know what Frost was talking about.

"Oh, I thought you were going?" Frost asked lightly as Blake walked back towards him.

"Kerry Nightingale?"

"You remember her, Mr Harte, don't insult my intelligence."

"Of course I remember her."

"The one that got away," Frost said in a singsong voice, looking up at Blake, the flickering light reflecting in his jet black eyes. "Or so she thought. So *you* thought. I came so tantalisingly close to throttling the life out of her, just like the others. But you got there *just* in time. Blake Harte, the white knight. The man who saves the damsels. But there's nothing you can do this time."

"You're bluffing," Blake told him. "There's nothing you can do trapped in here."

Again, Frost chuckled. "Oh, how little you know. She lives quite close to you these days, doesn't she? A woman in her position is well publicised. I've seen her on the news. Doing very well for herself. Local politician, I expect the people of Clackton are so very reassured that she's there, looking after them. But isn't it amazing how freely prey thinks it can move when it thinks it's safe? But she isn't. She hasn't been since I first clapped eyes on her all those years ago. Her day was always coming. Yes, Mr Harte. I *know* where she works. I *know* where she lives. I k*now* everything about her. Including when she's going to die. I just thought you'd like to know that. Put *that* in your interview records. Kerry Nightingale will be dead by the end of the week."

CHAPTER
TWO

Blake sat in his car and sucked on his ecig. Now he was out of the prison, he could allow himself to acknowledge how unsettled and freaked out he felt from seeing Frost again after so long. Throughout his career, Blake had been responsible for sending his fair share of killers to prison, but Thomas Frost was one he still had the occasional nightmare about.

Blake had heard rumblings from his old colleagues that Frost had wanted to see him, but he had always ignored them and now he was sincerely wishing he had continued doing just that. But something had finally made him relent and he was now cursing himself for being so stupid to give Frost what he wanted. Because it had clearly been his aim to unsettle Blake and he had achieved exactly that.

How did he know so much about Kerry Nightingale? It was certainly true that she had been well covered by the media in recent months. She had won her local election by a landslide and was now regaled as one of the best things that had ever happened to Clackton, the nearest town to Harmschapel. But the question Blake now needed to work out was whether she was in any real danger. Frost was held in a high security prison. There was absolutely no way he would be able to get out without being seen, but he was also one of the most intelligent men Blake had ever met. During the original case, Blake had spoken to several psychiatrists who had stated that everything he did and said was with precise and methodical reasoning. Blake put the keys in the ignition and drove out of the car park.

Try as he might, there was no way he was able to ignore Frost's threats. Arriving at a T-junction, he glanced up at the road sign in front of him. One direction pointed him back home to Harmschapel, the other towards Clackton. He tapped the steering wheel in an agitated fashion. As a large lorry pulled up behind Blake, waiting for him to get out of the way, he made a decision. He flicked his indicator and put his foot down. He was going to Clackton.

Kerry Nightingale lived in the exclusive area of Clackton. The apartments and houses were ranged from quite expensive to more a month than Blake earned in a year. As he arrived outside the Clayton apartments, he looked up at the building in front of him. It was a tall, towering structure that housed somewhere in the range of fifty apartments, the most expensive of which boasted balconies that allowed the owner to look down at the people below. A huge billboard on the side of the building showcasing the interior of some of the highest floored luxury apartments, demonstrating the sleek and modern marble kitchens and cosily lit living areas, along with beautifully tiled bathrooms, and enormous luxurious bedrooms caused Blake to sigh. He was rather fond of Juniper Cottage, his home in Harmschapel, but he had often wondered how it would feel to live somewhere like Clayton Apartments.

Locking his car, he hurried across the road to the main entrance and peered through the glass door into the reception area. Behind the desk was a young security guard, reading a paper and sipping from a drinks can. He looked up as Blake knocked on the glass. The guard frowned when he caught sight of Blake's police identification, pressing a button underneath his desk, which released the lock on the door, accompanied by a droning buzz as Blake opened the door and walked towards him.

"Can I help you?" he asked, putting his newspaper out of sight under the desk.

"Detective Sergeant Blake Harte. I'm looking for Kerry Nightingale. She *does* live here, doesn't she?"

The security guard's face dropped. "Yeah, she does," he replied flatly. "You've just missed her going up actually. One second."

He picked up a phone from behind the desk and put it to his ear as he quickly tapped on the keypad. "Kerry, it's Jamie from security. There's a man here to see you." He glanced up at Blake. "What was the name again?"

"DS Blake Harte."

"A Detective Sergeant Blake Harte," Jamie repeated into the phone. He paused then nodded. "Will do." He placed the phone back on the receiver and shook his head, exhaling in annoyance. "She'll be down in a minute. Though, I warn you. If you've come asking her to sort you lot out an extra tea break or something, she'll chew up to pieces."

Blake raised an eyebrow. "No, no, it's not about that."

Jamie shrugged and pulled his newspaper out from underneath the desk and resumed reading. Blake watched him while he waited for Kerry to come and meet him. Jamie was very handsome, in fact, Blake would even go as far to call him pretty. He had mousy brown hair that had clearly been straightened and visible through a gap in the top buttons of his shirt was a necklace with a ying and yang symbol in the centre.

"Worked here long?" Blake asked him lightly, to pass the time.

Jamie glanced up from his paper. "Me? No, not really. A few months. It's a pretty cushy job to be honest. There's a few of us on security, but they could probably do away with us altogether. There's barely anything to do. Still, I'm not complaining. The money is decent."

Blake nodded, but was slightly relieved when the lift bell rang and Kerry Nightingale stepped out. She was a slender bodied lady, with shoulder length brown hair, and a slightly pale complexion.

"Kerry?" Blake asked as she stepped into reception.

Kerry turned to face Blake and frowned. "Do I know you?"

"We have met before, yes," Blake replied delicately. "I was hoping to have a chat with you. I'm Detective Sergeant Blake Harte."

"I do hope you haven't come to try and twist my arm about anything," Kerry replied, her eyes narrowing. "I don't give personal meetings without an appointment."

"It's nothing like that, no," Blake said, glancing at

Jamie who was watching the conversation with mild interest. "I'm here on a slightly more official capacity."

Kerry's eyebrows suddenly shot up. "Just a minute," she said, pointing vaguely at him. "I *do* know you, don't I? Blake Harte, did you say your name was?"

"That's right," Blake said, ushering her back towards the lift before she fully remembered where she had seen him last. "Can we go somewhere more private?"

The look in Kerry's eyes told Blake that she was beginning to cotton on as to who he was, but she nodded, and with a last fervent glance at Jamie, she pressed the button on the elevator door. As the doors slid open, they stepped inside, and she stabbed the button to the top floor with her thumb.

"You're one of the officers who worked on the Thomas Frost case, aren't you?" she asked quietly, once the lift was moving, fear evident in her eyes.

"That's right," Blake replied.

"Why do you want to see me? I thought that was all over and done with? Is that what this is about?"

"It is, yes."

Kerry put her hands to her mouth as the lift reached the top floor. "He's escaped hasn't he?"

"No, I can categorically tell you that he *is* still in prison where he belongs, under constant observation," Blake said as the lift doors opened and they stepped out.

"Then why are you here?"

Blake took a deep breath, trying to decide how best to phrase what he was going to say. "He's been making threats. I know that might sound alarming, but you must be reassured that there is absolutely no way for him to get to you."

They reached the door to Kerry's apartment and walked inside. As the banner outside had promised, it was lush and spacious. The kitchen area was awash with black marble counters and a silver stained oven protruded out of the wall. Kerry walked straight to the fridge, which at first looked like another marble panel in the wall. Inside, Blake could see several bottles of white wine waiting to be opened, reminding him of the cider he had waiting for him back in Harmschapel.

"Looks like the fridge of my dreams," Blake remarked as Kerry removed a bottle and placed it on the counter.

Kerry gave him a small smile as she unscrewed the bottle. "I should be more careful really, with the medication I'm on, but you only live once, right? I would offer you one, but I assume you're driving."

Blake nodded as she poured herself a generous helping of the wine into a large glass and took a gulp, staring out towards the balcony, which was situated next to the living room.

"What threats has he been making?" she asked,

before taking another sip of wine.

Again, Blake considered his reply, but Kerry seemed to notice his hesitation. "Please don't try and pander to me, Mr Harte. I know better than anybody what that man is capable of. It wasn't you who was seconds away from having the life squeezed out of you." Perhaps instinctively she put her hands to her neck and rubbed it as she continued staring out of the window.

"He cannot touch you, Kerry, I want you to know that," Blake said, gauging her reaction. He could see no reason in placing unnecessary worry upon her. "But all I'm here to tell you is to just be vigilant. Any suspicious phone calls, mail, or somebody in the street, you report it. I'll even give you my card if you want to speak to me. But there's no reason for you to live your life any differently."

Kerry drained her wine glass and immediately poured another, even larger glass. Without another word, she walked across the kitchen and out onto the balcony. Blake debated for a moment as to whether he should just place his card on the counter and leave her in peace, but he found himself following her out onto the balcony.

Apart from a couple of potted plants, the only furniture was a small table with a few chairs. Kerry stared out over the edge with her back to Blake. The view from the balcony illustrated how high up her apartment was from the ground. The glass barrier and rail was the only block between them and a long drop to the bottom.

"You're in a very secure apartment," Blake said gently. "Lock that door at night and nobody can get to you."

"I'm stepping down from politics," Kerry replied, without turning round. "Every time I'm in front of a camera, giving an interview, or talking to the local paper, my mind is never on the job. It's always *him*. Right in *front* of me. *Watching*. I could be cutting a ribbon at a new playschool, all those happy children's faces all around me, and I'm not registering a single one of them."

"I promise you, you are *not* in any danger."

"Then why did you come here?"

"Because I see him too, Kerry. Not as much as you, I know, but he's still there. It takes time for evil like that to fade away. But he's been making threats directly about you."

Kerry took another large gulp of wine but remained silent.

"I can arrange for you to be protected-"

"'It's *over now*.'"

"Sorry?"

"That's what you said the last time we met. Just before I moved here." She turned to him, her eyes fearful. "*It's over now. He's locked away, he can't get to you.'* Now you're telling me I'm in danger even when he's in prison?"

"I'm just keeping you up to speed," Blake replied. "That's all. But like I said, I can get you protection."

Kerry nodded before downing the rest of her wine. "Don't tell me. Numerous police following me around everywhere, and camping outside my door? I don't think so, Mr Harte. When I'm in Clackton, I hold my head up high. It's what people expect. I will *not* be constantly looking over my shoulder. As for when I'm at home, I have a perfectly suitable security team working here. Kerry Nightingale, under police watch? The media would have a field day. And I presume it's me being in the public eye that has made him aware of me? He knows where I am. He must do, or you wouldn't be here now, would you?" she cried sharply. Blake paused, and then nodded.

"I have a friend who lives in Spain," Kerry said, turning back around to stare out over the balcony again. "I've done everything I want to do here. Manchester was too much. I was a small fish in a big pond as far as politics were concerned, especially after Brexit. But here, I could make my voice heard."

"You're moving to Spain?"

"At the end of the week," Kerry said, nodding. "I'm nearly fifty, Mr Harte. I don't want to spend the rest of my life doing this. Especially if Thomas Frost is still –" Her voice faded away, and Blake wondered if she might cry. Her public image was one of steely determination, so much so that the press had recently started calling her *'Clackton's Iron Lady,'* even though she represented a completely different party to the original *'Iron Lady'*. She turned to him, a resolute expression on her face. "I'm handing in my notice tomorrow. So, whatever Thomas Frost wants to do to me, he's not got very much time."

CHAPTER
THREE

The position of the security camera gave a clear view to Kerry's apartment because it had been placed in such a way that allowed it full vision of the corridor, including the door that Jamie had watched Blake and Kerry walk through once they had come out of the lift.

In truth, Jamie cursed himself whenever he found himself in this position; sat at the reception desk, staring idly at the screen, and it was not an unfamiliar feeling for him to be doing this while wondering what was going on behind her apartment door after he had observed her going in there with someone he had never seen before.

He drained the rest of the energy drink can and threw it towards the bin underneath the desk. It bounced off the corner and clattered onto the floor, but Jamie barely noticed. Instead, he continued watching the screen for any sign of movement that would signal that the mysterious meeting between the police officer and Kerry had come to an end.

As he leant back in the chair, never taking his eyes off the screen, he was only too aware of his pride, which still felt like it had taken a bit of a battering from Kerry's admonishment before she had stormed into the lift before Blake had arrived. His eyes narrowed slightly as her words rang round his ears. *'Get over yourself Jamie, for God's sake. You think you're the first? Grow up.'*

It had been two weeks since she had broken up with him, for reasons she clearly felt no need to specify and now all Jamie could do with himself on a day-to-day basis was sit and seethe in resentment.

His thoughts were broken by the sound of the entrance door buzzer as it pushed open and his colleague, Sonia Carmichael, walked in, her huge frame brushing the threshold of the door. Jamie glanced up at her as she punched the sequence into the keypad on the reception office door.

"*Evening*," Sonia said, dumping her rucksack in

the corner of the office and throwing herself down on a chair. It creaked underneath her large backside. "You alright?"

Jamie grunted in reply, his eyes returning to the screen and Kerry's apartment door at the end of the top floor corridor.

Sonia tutted loudly and bent down to pick up the empty energy drink can, throwing it into the bin pointedly. "Three inches away from the bin, Jamie, for God's sake. It's not like you've had anything *better* to do." She glanced up at the screen and rolled her eyes. "There's a point where that goes from puppy dog to just creepy, you know."

"So she tells me," Jamie muttered, turning to face Sonia for the first time. Her brown matted hair was plastered across her forehead, the energy required from her short walk to work from her student flat a few streets away evident from the beads of sweat visible on her forehead. She rolled her eyes.

"You *do* realise there are plenty of women out there who would kill to get with someone like you?" She looked at him with that same simpering expression she always did.

Jamie was in no mood for her fawning over him. "Yeah, well maybe *I* don't want *them*."

"And *she* doesn't want *you*," Sonia snapped, opening her rucksack and pulling out one of her crime novels that she always read when she was meant to be working. "Maybe try getting *that* into your head." She threw herself back onto the swivel chair again, and buried her nose in the book.

When Jamie had started working at the apartment blocks, it had not taken long for him to become aware of how much Sonia fancied him. Subtlety was in no way her strong point. She had frequently arranged for her shifts to cross over with his so she could spend a bit of extra time telling him how nice he looked or gather as much information as Jamie chose to give her about his personal life. Jamie did not like to think of himself as a shallow sort of person, but he could not help but feel a slight sense of condescension towards her for thinking he was anywhere close to in her league. Whilst Jamie was athletic, toned, and attractive, Sonia was short, very overweight and always seemed to smell of slightly stale sweat. Jamie could sympathise as there had been a time in his life when he had been the Sonia of his friendship groups; constantly grasping onto anything that resembled attraction from any girl – whether the feeling was mutual or not – until the day had come when he had decided to do something about it. Two years of gyms and a complete change of diet later, and he was the one who was now able to secretly smirk at the less fortunate in love.

His eyes darted back to the screen as the door of Kerry's apartment finally opened and she and Blake stepped out and began walking back to the lift.

"I take it she's had a man up there?" Sonia asked flatly, not looking up from her book.

"Yeah. They're coming down now," Jamie said, quickly pushing his chair away from the screen. "And don't start throwing in all your funny comments when she's down here, alright?"

"Don't know what you mean, Jamie," Sonia replied. "I just think it's pretty sad to watch you clinging onto something that's never going to happen."

"You'd know all about that, wouldn't you?" he spat back at her.

Before Sonia could reply, the lift doors opened, and Blake and Kerry stepped out. As they walked towards the desk, Jamie watched the expression on Kerry's face. She looked serious, remaining silent as Blake arrived at the desk.

"Is it just you two here from security at the moment?" he asked.

Jamie nodded, still unsure as to whether Blake was somebody he ought to feel threatened by or not. Judging by how distant Kerry looked, he did not think that Blake was like any of the other men that Kerry had had up in her room the past few weeks.

"Hello there," Blake said to Sonia who was looking up at him, clueless. "I'm DS Blake Harte." He produced his ID and Sonia's eyes widened. Blake did not seem to notice and as he put his ID back in his pocket, he glanced at Kerry. "We – well, *I* – have become aware of some threats being made against Miss Nightingale. Now, I have offered some police protection, but Kerry feels that security here is sufficient enough. So, can I ask, and I'll pop in again to talk to your security manager, that extra vigilance is taken by you guys in regards to Kerry's safety?"

Sonia put her book down and stared at Blake bewildered. "How are we supposed to protect her from any threats when she isn't here? We're security, not body guards."

"Honestly, Sonia, there's really no need to worry about me," Kerry murmured. "Mr Harte is just doing his job."

"All the same," Blake replied. "I would ask that you and anybody else on security really keep an eye on Kerry until she leaves next week."

Jamie's head turned quickly to Kerry. "Leaving? What do you mean you're leaving? Where are you going?"

Kerry closed her eyes and sighed heavily. "Jamie, *please*."

"Where are you going though?" Jamie pressed.

"Spain," Kerry said to him sharply. "Not that it's *anything t*o do with you." She turned to Blake and gestured towards the door. "Thanks for dropping by, Mr Harte. I'll be sure to call you if I have any problems."

Blake glanced between Kerry and Jamie for a

moment then nodded. "You've got my card upstairs. Take care." He nodded towards Jamie and then Sonia, who was looking at Blake with the same simpering expression she usually reserved for Jamie, and walked out of the door.

Jamie barely noticed him leave. He was now standing and glaring at Kerry. "You were just going to leave without telling me?"

Kerry let out an exasperated moan. "Why would I tell you anything Jamie? *Why?* Let me spell it out for you – you are the *last* thing on my mind at the moment. Just grow up, for God's sake!"

And with that, she stormed back towards the lift. Jamie shook his head in disbelief. How could she be so callous towards him?

Sonia chuckled to herself as she picked up her book again. "I stand corrected. Carry on pursuing her. I think you're really in with a chance there."

Jamie wasn't listening. As he turned back to the security screens, his eyes narrowed as Kerry appeared on the top floor corridor. An array of images of her sunning herself with numerous men flashed through Jamie's brain. He had decided when he had first joined a gym that the days of people treating him badly were long behind him. Kerry Nightingale was no exception. She was not going to get away with how she had spoken to him, he decided. If he could not have Kerry, he was going to make sure that nobody else could either.

CHAPTER FOUR

As Blake had expected, by the time he arrived home to Juniper Cottage, his boyfriend, Harrison was already waiting for him.

The evening was drawing in, and as Blake pulled up beside his cottage, the beam from his headlights illuminated Harrison's blonde hair and smiling face. The sight of him instantly made Blake feel more relaxed, and as he pulled the keys out of the ignition, he returned the smile and climbed out of the car.

"Evening," Harrison said, walking towards him

and kissing him. "Are you alright?"

"It's been a hell of day," Blake replied, as he unlocked the door to his cottage.

They walked inside and Harrison closed the door behind him. "Where have you been? I went to the station but they said you'd left early to go and see someone?"

Blake nodded as he walked through to the kitchen to flick on the kettle. "Actually," he said, changing his mind. "I need something stronger. Do you fancy a beer?"

"Yeah, why not?" Harrison looked at him with a concerned look as he took the beer that Blake offered him out the fridge. He pulled it open and said, "What's happened? Who did you go to see?"

Blake sighed and nodded towards the living room, indicating that Harrison should follow him. They sat down on the sofa and Blake took his ecig out of his pocket, inhaling deeply on it before continuing.

"I don't know if you'd have seen it on the news, but seven years ago, do you remember there being a massive story about a serial killer in the Manchester area? Jack Frost?"

Harrison frowned. "No?"

"His name is actually Thomas Frost, but far be it from the media to miss the opportunity of a pun to splash across their front pages in place of any facts." Blake took a swig from his beer can. "Thomas Frost was the biggest case I have ever worked on. From 2009 to 2010, he killed five women, all of them strangled. He led us on a wild goose chase all 'round the city, just picking off his victims, apparently at random. He was *clever* – always cleaned up the crime scenes, any clues we found as to who he might be were because he wanted us to find them. Finally, we caught him. We got a call from a concerned neighbour of his next to be victim about a suspicious man lurking around the property. Turned out he didn't like successful women. According to Frost, there wasn't a woman alive that shouldn't be living in his shadow. So, any woman in the city that he saw as above herself, he targeted." He took another long sip of beer, hoping that some of the anxiety from his day would diminish. "I've seen some crazy things in this job. Things you have to learn to just live with. Some people are just messed up in the head, and the results can be brutal. But I've never met anyone quite as cold and callous as Frost. He just didn't care. He liked his victims scared."

Harrison leant forward, cradling his beer can. "Okay. So, why are you telling me this?"

"I went to see him." Blake murmured.

"Who? Thomas Frost?"

"Yeah."

"*Why?*" Harrison exclaimed, staring at Blake, eyes wide.

"He's been asking to see me for ages," Blake

replied. "And I've always ignored him. A few months before I left Manchester, he was sending me letters, constantly requesting that I give him ten minutes of my time. The other day, another letter arrived here."

Harrison's eyes widened. "What? He knows where you live?"

"No, I don't think so." Blake shook his head. "They'd have just sent any mail on to me from my old post, they wouldn't have known what it was. But Frost is a clever man. He's persistent. And he knew that I wouldn't be able to resist."

He walked across to a chest of drawers in the corner of the living room and pulled open the top one, producing a letter and holding it in the air. "According to him, we have *'unfinished business.'*"

"You and him?"

Blake explained what had happened that day, how Frost had made a promise that Kerry Nightingale would be dead by the end of the week, that he, Blake, had gone to see Kerry and tried to tell her what was going on and how she had reacted. When he was finished, he sat back down next to Harrison and put his head in his hands. "She said she's moving to Spain at the end of the week anyway, and that she doesn't believe she's in any danger. But I'm not convinced she's not."

Harrison put his hand on Blake's arm. "If this guy is in prison, how is he supposed to get to her? He's under lock and key."

Blake shook his head again. Try as he might, he could not shake the feeling that something awful was going to happen. "I saved Kerry Nightingale's life seven years ago. We forced our way into her house just as Frost was throttling the life out of her. I dragged him off, and arrested him there and then for the murders of all the other women. Even then, when it was all over, we knew we had our man and he knew we'd got him. He looked me straight in the eye that night and said '*I'll get her one day.*' Now, seven years later, and he's saying exactly the same thing."

"He's a psycho, Blake," Harrison reasoned. "He's going to say things like that. You've got nothing to worry about." He put his arm around Blake and pulled him in tight. "He's in prison and she's in a flat with a security team and people around her all the time. She's safe. There's nothing he could possibly do."

Blake looked Harrison right in the eyes. "Then why am I so convinced that she isn't going to survive the week?"

Harrison did not seem to be able to think of a reply. He just pulled Blake in tighter, and despite everything that was happening, Blake felt a little reassured. Since they had met, Harrison had been through more than most people his age would have to deal with in two lifetimes. Two of his ex-partners were dead, one murdered, one by jumping off the church roof. Blake had been involved in all of this, and just two months ago, they had both come face to face with Blake's ex, whilst another crazy murder had gone on around them. Despite the emotional rollercoaster that had been their relationship, they both knew that it had been the reason they were now together. And as they sat in silence on the sofa, Blake knew it had all been worth it.

He had been thinking about how he wanted to phrase what he was about to say, but as the moment arrived, his words came out simply and without any inner turmoil. "Move in."

Harrison looked down at him, his expression soft. "Hmm?"

Blake sat up and took a hold of his hand. "Move in here. Sell the cottage and move in with me."

Harrison looked surprised. "*Really?*"

"Yeah. Why not? It's the next step, right? We practically live with each other anyway, I'm always at yours, and you're always here. We might as well make it permanent?"

For one horrible moment, Blake thought that Harrison was going to decline, but instead his face broke out into a delighted grin and he nodded. "Alright. Let's do it."

Blake smiled back at him and pulled him in for a kiss. After a moment, Harrison pulled away. "There's one problem though."

"What?"

Harrison grimaced. "Betty."

Blake closed his eyes and groaned. Somehow, he had managed to forget about Harrison's rambunctious goat that he had owned since he was a child. Betty, it seemed, absolutely hated Blake. "Couldn't you add her in as an extra on the cottage? Advertise her as onsite security?"

Harrison chuckled. "No. Come on Blake, I know it seems stupid to you, but she was pretty much my only friend when I was growing up. When everything was happening with Daniel and my parents were…" he hesitated and shook his head. "…doing their thing, Betty was the one who distracted me. I can't just abandon her."

Blake sighed. "No, I know. We'll sort something out. The thing is, I can't have her in the house. I sometimes bring work home with me and I can't have the details of confidential cases going down her gullet."

"I set up a little shed for her in my yard. All we need to do is put it out the front. We'll take her for walks, it'll be fine."

Blake raised an eyebrow. "Take her for walks? She's a goat."

"It's not about the walk," Harrison laughed. "The point of taking a goat out is the brush-eating they do while they're walking. Saves on money for food and gives her a bit of stimulation instead of being cooped in a shed all day."

Blake sighed and shook his head with amusement. "And that's the deal? You'll move in as long as Betty is happy with her living arrangements and daily exertions?"

Harrison nodded. "That's the deal."

"Then how about," Blake said, placing his beer can down on the ground before standing up and pulling Harrison to his feet, "that we make that official?"

Harrison followed Blake's glance towards the stairs and grinned. "We'll talk goat sheds afterwards, yes?"

"Yeah, sure, promise," Blake said vaguely, leading him towards the stairs. He flicked off the light and the cottage plunged into darkness as he led his boyfriend towards the bedroom.

Blake was not sure what woke him a few hours later but as he looked at the clock on his bedside table, which read two AM, he suddenly felt wide-awake. Beside him, Harrison softly snored into the pillow, so Blake gently got out of bed and pulled on a pair of jogging bottoms.

His thoughts immediately returned to Thomas Frost and his would-be victim, as if the passion with Harrison before they had fallen asleep had merely paused his brain. Despite Harrison's reassurances that it was surely impossible for Frost to get to Kerry at all,

Blake could not shake off the feeling that there was a reason why Frost had been so keen to tell him what he had.

His throat began to feel dry so Blake tiptoed across the bedroom, cringing slightly at the creak of floorboards beneath his bare feet. He made his way downstairs to the kitchen and poured himself a glass of water. He stared out of the window, deep in thought as he slowly sipped it. He could not get the image of Thomas Frost out of his head, sneering at him, seven years ago when he had been pulled off Kerry and arrested, vowing that it was not the end.

Blake wandered into the living room, smiling at the sight of Harrison's trainers by the door. It was an addition to the room that he was only too happy to start getting used to. After everything that had happened, it felt like they had finally earned this moment.

The sound of a car approaching outside broke his thoughts. Anywhere else Blake had ever lived, the sound of a car at this time of night would not have even registered, but in Harmschapel, traffic was a rare thing after a certain time, and non-existent at this hour.

A few moments later, the car came to a stop with the engine running, right outside his cottage. Blake was just about to lean over the sofa and peer out of the curtains when there was a loud metallic thud on the front door.

In the time it took for Blake to jump up and unlock the door, the sound of screeching tyres filled the air, and when he opened the door the smell of burning rubber filled his nostrils. In the distance, he could just make out the back red lights of the car shining in the darkness. But then, Blake saw what had made the sound on the door. There was a large carving knife stuck in the wood, holding a sheet of paper in place.

As he stared at it, Blake vaguely heard Harrison run down the stairs behind him.

"What was that?" Harrison murmured, rubbing his eyes. "Did I hear a car?"

Blake couldn't answer him. He was transfixed on the paper on the door. It was a picture of Kerry Nightingale, smiling proudly at the camera, sunglasses making her appear cool and collected, shaking hands with another MP, at the height of her political career, and below the picture, in bright red writing: *'SHE'LL BE DEAD BY MORNING.'*

CHAPTER
FIVE

Jamie closed his eyes as he hurtled towards the ground, his feet having given out from underneath him as he had stumbled home from the club, drunker than he had been for quite a long time.

His face whacked the side of the pavement and he let out a moan as the sound of laughter and jeering from other drunken revellers echoed around him. He ignored them, pulled himself up off the ground, grabbing hold of a lamppost for support, and continued stumbling down the road.

It had not been the greatest of days. After Kerry had snubbed him again, Jamie had left work in an absolutely foul mood with the one aim of getting himself as drunk as he possibly could with the thirty pound he had left over in his account before pay day. As it was, the first bar he had walked into had one pound drinks on offer and before too long, he had found himself getting into a fight which had resulted in him being forcibly removed from the bar.

If it had not been for Kerry constantly at the forefront of his mind, Jamie would have hung around the bar in order to give the other man who he had been fighting with a second round, but instead he was now stumbling down the road towards the apartment building where not only did he work, but she lived.

As the apartment block came into view, Jamie remembered when he and Kerry had first met. She had just moved into the apartments and he had been helping her haul a lot of bags and boxes towards the lift after the delivery men had driven off without helping, more than likely because Kerry had been chastising them for the way in which they had been handling her belongings. They had started chatting and before too long, Jamie had become completely entranced by her. Something about her had occupied his feelings from that day forwards, and at first it felt entirely mutual. Because of her political career, Kerry had insisted that their relationship was undertaken very much on the quiet, something Jamie was only too happy to oblige with. A week ago, that had all changed. She had gone from doting and romantic to cold and distant, culminating in her telling him she wanted their relationship to end. She had not even had the good grace to explain why, just that she felt that they *'had gone as far as they could.'*

Jamie arrived at the entrance to the apartments. Through the glass, he could see Sonia sitting in one of the chairs behind the desk with her feet up, still engrossed in one of her crime novels, her huge frame bulging out over the side of her chair, looking as sweaty and out of breath as ever.

Jamie banged on the glass angrily, leaning against the wall. Sonia glanced up at him and stared in surprise before pressing the release button underneath the desk.

"What are you doing here?" she asked as he stumbled through the door.

"I wanna speak to Kerry," Jamie slurred, storming past her and towards the lift.

"Jamie, it's three in the morning for God's sake," Sonia replied, slamming her book down. "Look at the state of you – go home and sober yourself up."

Jamie ignored her. He punched the button to call the lift and it opened immediately. Before Sonia could reach him to try and pull him out, the doors were closing and he was on his way up to the top floor.

"This better be important, Jamie," Kerry snapped, standing in the doorway, a furious look in her eyes.

"Of course it's important," Jamie slurred, pushing past her. "That is, *I* think it's important anyway. I thought *we* were important, turns out I was wrong."

Kerry sighed and closed the flat door. "I would offer you a drink, but it looks like you've had enough already."

"*You* don't have the *right* to judge *me*."

"Just say what you came to say and get out. I have things to do."

"Yeah," Jamie scoffed, glaring at her. "Like running away to Spain? Got some Spanish guy to keep you, have you?"

"That's none of your business, Jamie. Now, are we done here?"

"*No!*" Jamie shouted, the vast amount of beer he had drank intensifying his emotions. "Before you run away, -"

"I am *not* running away."

"I want to know why you ended things between us."

Kerry rolled her eyes. "Because you're a child, Jamie. I'm old enough to be your mother. We would never have worked."

"Yeah?" Jamie snarled, storming towards the bedroom door and kicking it open. "Didn't seem to bother you when we were both on that bed, did it?"

He flicked the light switch to the bedroom on but nothing happened other than a quiet crack as the bulb blew.

Kerry glanced at the light with a slight air of derision. "Maybe I'm going to move to somewhere where the lights don't need replacing every five minutes?"

Jamie slammed the door to the pitch-black bedroom and pointed an accusing finger at her. "Do y'know what? I hope you meet someone who you really like, someone you really fall for –"

"Don't be *dramatic*, Jamie. You didn't fall for me."

"Yes I did. Don't tell me how I felt," he snapped furiously. He could feel a lump in his throat and became even angrier at the fact that he was close to bursting into tears. "And I hope you meet someone who you fall for and they break your heart in the same way you did mine – I hope it absolutely destroys you."

"Lovely, Jamie. Really mature. I was totally wrong about you. Now, please, get out. And don't bother me again."

Jamie stared at her in disbelief. "You *really* are a *heartless* cow, you know that?"

Kerry didn't reply. She just opened the door to the flat and held it open, staring nonchalantly at the ceiling.

Jamie's fists clenched. All day he had been

thinking about how he could punish her for how she had made him feel. She had humiliated him, thrown him away like a piece of rubbish. There was nothing more he wanted to do at this moment than give her even half the amount of pain she had given him. He could do anything to her in this flat. If he managed to get that door closed, there would be no way of anyone getting to her before it was too late. He took a step towards her and contemplated as to whether he was really about to lash out at her when his eyes landed on a leaflet lying on the coffee table. At first he thought he had misread what was written on the front but as he looked closer, he realised what it said.

Kerry followed his eye line and ran towards the leaflet in horror, but Jamie pushed her out the way, sending her flying into a cabinet.

"Jamie, don't, -"

But he barely heard her. He just picked up the leaflet and stared at it. "*Abortion?*" he said quietly.

Kerry closed her eyes and looked down at the ground.

He stared at her, questions ricocheting around his head, none of which he was sure he wanted to hear the answers to. "You're pregnant?"

Again Kerry didn't answer. She just looked up from the ground, first at him then back to the leaflet again.

Jamie's heart ached. "You *were* pregnant?"

Still, Kerry remained silent.

Jamie looked down at the leaflet helplessly, as if it were about to produce some of the information she wasn't giving him.

"I'm sorry. I didn't want you to find out this way."

"You didn't want me to find out *at all!*" he shouted back at her. "I was going to be a *father? And you didn't tell me?* How could you not *tell me?*" He stormed towards her, a red mist transcending. But just as he was about to raise his fist to strike her, a loud voice stopped him in his tracks.

"*Jamie!*" It was Sonia. She was standing in the still open doorway, staring at the situation with concern. "I think you'd better go, don't you?"

For a moment, Jamie considered completely ignoring her and continuing trying to attack Kerry. But even in his livid and drunken frame of mind, he realised how stupid it would be to do it in front of a witness. Instead, he screwed up the leaflet, which was still in his hand, and flung it at Kerry, who was now cowering by the door. "You're *scum*," he spat. "And you *will* pay for this. I *promise* you that."

Without another word, Jamie pushed past Sonia and stormed down the corridor.

CHAPTER SIX

The journey was not an especially long one, but the country roads leading to Clackton seemed more bendy and difficult to navigate than ever before, especially with the urgency Blake felt as he put his foot down. He was desperate to get to Clayton Apartments as quickly as he could.

The poster on the door had unnerved Blake. He had racked his brains to think who could have left him the ominous note on his door but had come to no real conclusions. Someone like Frost would know plenty of people who were capable of anything, there were groups of people he had seen while working in the city that still made his skin crawl to think about. But how would they have known where to go to leave a threat on his door? Did he now have members of Frost's circles watching his every move? His mind briefly flicked to Harrison, alone in Juniper Cottage, more than likely back in bed, with no real way of getting help. He pushed the unpleasant notions out of his head. All he could concentrate on now was making sure that the promises on the sheet of paper that he could almost feel burning his leg in his pocket could not come to pass.

There was a fork in the road that had long since been described by local residents as an extremely unsafe area for drivers. Its main problem was a blind spot from Blake's approaching perspective to anything coming from the left hand side until he was right in the centre of it, and sure enough, much to Blake's disbelief, as he arrived at the centre, he saw a car that had come off the road. It was on its side in a ditch, the horn blaring constantly. Through the front window screen Blake could see that the airbags had been deployed. Regardless of the situation, there was no way Blake could just drive by without stopping to help, so he screeched to a halt beside the road and jumped out his car.

The horn continued blaring as Blake stumbled down the embankment to the driver's side and peered through the window. The driver was motionless, his face in the air bag. The smell of rubber in the air told him that the accident could only have happened in the past few minutes. Blake sighed and pulled his phone out of his pocket to call for an ambulance, pulling the car door open.

"Hello? Can you hear me, mate?" There was no response.

Blake reached behind the man's head to feel for a pulse. To his relief, he traced one. But as he explained the situation to the operator on the phone, the faint whiff of whiskey hit him. Any sympathy he felt for the driver soon diminished as he realised that had probably been drunk.

The ambulance soon arrived and Blake took down the details on where to speak to the driver when he regained consciousness. As he watched the driver being loaded into the ambulance on a stretcher, he glanced at his phone. He had wasted too much time getting to Kerry. He climbed into his car and drove as quickly as he could to Clayton Apartments.

At this time of night, even in a busy town like Clackton, all was silent and still. Only the faint echo of a group of drunk men tottering out of a kebab shop a few streets away could be heard as Blake screeched to a halt and jumped out of the car. He ran towards the building.

Glancing through the glass door and seeing nobody at the reception desk, Blake held his finger down on the bell to Kerry's apartment in desperation. After an agonising few moments, there was finally an answer.

"Who the hell is this at this time of night?"

Blake let out a sigh of relief at the sound of Kerry's irritated voice.

"Kerry, it's DS Harte. I'm sorry to bother you so late but I really need to speak to you quite urgently. Could I come in?"

"Oh, why not?" Kerry replied sarcastically through the intercom. "Everyone else seems to be doing!"

When Blake arrived at the top floor, he was surprised to see Sonia just on her way out of the flat.

"What are you doing here at this time?" Sonia asked him as Blake approached her.

"I could do with your help actually," Blake replied. He knocked on the door and waited for Kerry to answer. When she did, she looked extremely annoyed. She was wearing a long pink silk dressing gown that flowed down the floor.

"What is it? I am leaving tomorrow. I have to be up in a few hours, Mr Harte."

"I'm aware of that, Kerry. I'm sorry. But I've been made aware of some more threats against you."

"What threats? I'm going to be in Spain by this time tomorrow. What harm could I possibly come to?"

Blake debated showing her the notice but decided against it. "I think, just to be on the safe side, you should really let me get some back up to keep watch over you till you go, just for your own protection."

Kerry exhaled and put her hand on her hip. "Mr Harte. As I said to you yesterday, I have no wish to have a load of police surrounding me till I leave. I just can't be doing with it. Whoever is sending these threats is just after attention. I've had people sending me death threats ever since I went into politics, it's the nature of the beast."

"All the same, Miss Nightingale," Sonia ventured. "Would Mr Harte be here if he wasn't worried? This is a bit different from some saddo behind a keyboard giving you hassle on Twitter."

Kerry sighed, pinching between her eyes.

"How about if I stay outside your apartment for the rest of the night?" Sonia suggested. "That way, you've got the best of both worlds. No psycho is going to get past me, and you're on the top floor. This door is the only way to you."

Blake was not thrilled with the prospect of Sonia being the only form of protection but when Kerry nodded, he realised it was the only option she was willing to accept.

"Well, I'll stay here too," Blake said. "The type of people these could be are a bit more dangerous than your average security guard is used to dealing with, no offence."

Sonia shrugged.

"Fine, whatever you think," Kerry said, waving her hand dismissively. "But could I please get back to bed now?"

"Yes, just as soon as I've given your apartment a quick check," Blake replied. "It won't take a minute."

Kerry held her door open further with another resigned sigh.

Blake walked inside and searched all the rooms thoroughly for any place that someone might be hiding – in wardrobes, under the bed, and he even made sure that there was no way anybody could be hiding in the ceiling. After one last look on the balcony and a glance down to the long drop below, he was satisfied that there was nobody else in the apartment, other than Kerry.

"We'll be just outside," he said to her. "I have my phone, I can get back up here as quickly as is needed. And tomorrow, I will drive you to the airport. Okay?"

Kerry still looked annoyed with him, but her expression softened. "You're really worried about this, aren't you? You think I'm in actual danger?"

"Not now you're not," Blake said firmly. "I *promise* you. Nothing can happen to you now. See you in the morning."

"I'll be getting up at eight," Kerry said as he stepped out of the apartment.

"See you then. You're safe." Blake replied.

Kerry nodded and closed the door. Sonia raised her eyebrows and shrugged. "I guess we'll be needing some coffee then?"

Blake rubbed his eyes as he leant back in his chair, the caffeine from the strong coffee that Sonia had brought losing its effect with every passing moment.

"You really don't have to be here with me you know," he said to her. "I could have just blown this all out of proportion."

Sonia glanced up from her crime novel. It was one Blake had seen in Harmschapel's bookshop but had put it back on the shelf, as it had sounded too grizzly for his personal tastes. "You don't think you have though, do you? It's fine, I don't mind. I've got my phone should anybody ring the door downstairs, and anyway, I like Kerry. Plus, there's nothing to do downstairs. It's a rare night I have to ever leave the front desk so it makes a nice change."

Blake shrugged and nodded. They had been sat outside the door to Kerry's apartment for nearly two hours now. In another three hours, Kerry would be waking up and Blake could drive her to the airport, where she would be flying out of harm's way.

"Do you and Kerry talk much?" Blake asked her. "It's just that you were coming out of here when I arrived."

"Oh, I was just changing the light bulb in her room," Sonia replied, taking a sip of the coffee by her chair, which by now must have been stone cold. "Between you and me, the light bulbs they send us for the apartments only last about five minutes. We've told them no end of times, but you know what these conglomerate companies are like. Couldn't care less about the little people, so long as their money is coming in. Seem to spend my life sorting out light bulbs. I used to work in the club at the other end of town."

"As a DJ?"

"No, just a technician really. Changing all the bulbs above the dance floor, mucking about with the speakers, that sort of thing.

"But yeah, I do talk to Kerry a fair amount. She's a nice woman. Strictly off the record, she had a bit of a thing going with one of the lads on security. You met him, Jamie."

Blake raised his eyebrows. "I thought I detected a bit of a weird vibe between them."

"Weird is right," Sonia replied, rolling her eyes. "They were going out for a few months, then she put an end to it. Can't say I blame her. Jamie can be a bit clingy to say the least. I dunno why, he's gorgeous. He could probably have anybody he wanted."

"Holding a bit of a torch for him yourself?" Blake asked her lightly.

Sonia sighed. "I wouldn't say no obviously, but to be honest I'd be happy to have anybody these days." She picked up her book and straightened out the pages. "Been a long time since I've done anything like *that*."

Blake took in the young girl sat next to him. She seemed to be somebody who could be a very pretty woman who had, at some point, completely let herself go. She was quite overweight, her hair messy and her clothes creased. There was also the unmistakable whiff of sweat about her.

"There's somebody out there for everyone," he decided to say. "Some people can get it with the click of their fingers, and I always hated them, believe me. But then, someone can come along and just sweep you off your feet. I've got my partner moving in with me soon and believe me, that wasn't a relationship I saw coming. And I love him. I'd absolutely kill for him. How old are you?"

"Twenty seven," she murmured. She had the expression of someone who had been told all this before, perhaps to the point where she did not believe it to be true anymore.

"You're young yet," Blake told her. "I'm only thirty, there's a hell of a lot of your life to go yet. Keep your chin up."

"Which one?" she said, causing Blake to laugh, though he wasn't sure whether she was just being humourlessly self-deprecating or just critical of herself.

As the hours ticked by, Blake's eyes began to itch with tiredness, to the point where he was not sure whether he was safe to just drive back to Harmschapel, let alone take Kerry all the way to the airport. But he was determined to see his post through to the very end, even if it meant getting a taxi for Kerry in the process.

He chatted idly with Sonia as the morning drew closer but by the time it was nearly eight AM, he was seriously starting to struggle.

"Why don't you go and get some more coffee?" Sonia suggested, glancing at her watch. "Knowing Kerry like I do, she'll be jumping straight in the shower when she wakes up anyway. She won't be ready to go for about another half hour yet."

Blake glanced at his phone to check the time for himself. It only had one percent of battery left but it was able to tell him that it was a minute to eight.

"There's a camera trained on this door in the office anyway," Sonia said, throwing her now finished book down on the floor and stretching her arms. "You'll be able to see everything from there. I should know. I've seen Jamie sit and watch it for ages." She shook her head. "He needs to get a grip, honestly."

Blake toyed with his options, reasoning that he was hardly going to be able to shadow Kerry whilst she was showering. "Alright," he said at last.

Sonia pulled her keys out from her pocket, which

were attached to her waist by a clip with a long piece of elastic. "That's the key to the office. You might have to wiggle it about a bit in the lock."

From inside the apartment, they heard the sound of Kerry's alarm clock. "There you go," Sonia said, as she passed him the key to the office. "You might want to wash your face with some cold water. Always worked for me when I needed a bit of an extra bit of energy to get my essays done at uni."

Blake yawned as he took the key off her and walked back down the corridor to the lift. When he reached it, he pressed the button and the doors slid open. "Do you want anything?" he called to Sonia.

"Just a black tea will do me, thanks," she called back.

But then, just as the lift doors began to close on Blake, they heard a crash from inside the apartment. Sonia stood up and stared at the door. She pulled her keys out and jammed them in the lock to Kerry's door. "*Kerry?*"

Blake put his foot in the lift door and pulled it open as quickly as he could. By the time he had sprinted down the corridor to the door of the apartment, Sonia had already opened the door and ran inside.

Once they were in, Blake frantically looked around him. *"Kerry?"* he shouted.

"Check the bathroom," Sonia told him urgently as

she ran towards the bedroom.

Blake barged into the bathroom. Like the rest of the flat, it was sleek and modern but there was no sign of Kerry.

"Blake, she's in here!" Sonia called from the bedroom.

His heart pounding, Blake hurried across the flat to the bedroom where he saw Sonia on her knees over Kerry, who was lying on the floor.

"Blake, she's choking!" Sonia cried fearfully.

The bedroom curtains were closed but as Sonia pulled them open, the daylight streamed through the windows and illuminated the horror of Kerry. She was convulsing on the floor, her whole body shaking, and around her neck, the unmistakable imprint of a wire of some sort that had dug into her skin.

Blake pulled his phone out of his pocket to call for an ambulance but as he pressed the final '9,' to his dismay, the screen went black, having finally ran out of battery.

"*My phone's dead!*" he cried.

"I'll go use the phone downstairs," Sonia said, her voice shaking and more sweat than ever glistening on her forehead.

She quickly stepped over them and hurried out of the apartment as Kerry continued to convulse on the floor, but her body was now weakening. Desperately, Blake checked for a pulse, for any sign that she still had some fight left in her, but already he could tell that the life was slowly ebbing away from her.

"Come on, Kerry," he murmured. "Stay with me. You *have* to."

But her eyes had already glazed over. In the few minutes that it took for Sonia to burst back through the door, two burly paramedics behind her, Blake could tell that Kerry Nightingale was already dead.

CHAPTER
SEVEN

The flash of the forensic team's camera filled the room as they carefully examined Kerry's body. Blake was standing in the doorway to the bedroom, watching proceedings. He felt absolutely numb. The last words he had said to Kerry before she had closed the door of her apartment for the last time had been *'you're safe.'* Yet a few hours later, she was lying on her bedroom floor, the life squeezed out of her.

Sharon Donahue, the head forensic pathologist who Blake had worked with in cases like this since he had arrived in Harmschapel stood up from where she had been crouched down examining the thin line around Kerry's neck.

"Difficult to say exactly what was used," she said, looking down at the body. "But it's clearly a wire or a rope of some sort. Obviously we'll know more once we've got her back to base, but strangulations tend to be from behind. The assailant sneaks up behind the victim and throttles them that way, having taken them by surprise."

Blake closed his eyes, all too aware of how similar it sounded to what Thomas Frost had done to his victims. "Have you got a time of death?"

"Well, if you say you heard a crash in here at eight this morning, so about an hour or so ago, I wouldn't be able to argue with you."

"I don't get it," Blake murmured. "How? How did he get to her?"

"Judging by the state of her bedside table, I'd guess all this coming down to the floor is what caused the crash you head," Sharon continued. She was pointing to a now broken glass, a small mirror and a pile of books that were all on the floor, perhaps dragged down by Kerry as she had gone down.

"Would you say it was a struggle?" Blake asked her, his eyes drifting back to the body on the floor again.

"Difficult to say."

Blake felt a tap on his shoulder. Behind him stood PC Billy Mattison, one of the young constables at the station. "Doesn't look like the balcony's been touched, Sir. The door to it was locked when we got here, and even when we'd got it open, there's no way anybody would be able to get out that way. We're on the top floor and the drop down to the ground is way too high to climb down, let alone jump."

"So, here we are again," drawled another voice from the doorway. It was Sergeant Michael Gardiner. Ever since Blake had lived in Harmschapel, the pair of them had never seen eye to eye, mainly because when Blake had arrived, he had taken the post that Gardiner had been after for years. Aside from that, Gardiner was just a naturally prickly and irritating person. "Who is she?" he asked, glancing down at Kerry's body disdainfully.

"Her name is Kerry Nightingale," Blake replied curtly.

"And what's happened to her?"

"If you'd been here on time, Michael, you would know." Blake turned on his heels and went out onto the balcony, pulling his ecig straight out of his pocket, ignoring Gardiner's mutterings behind him.

He leant over the railings and looked down. Mattison was absolutely right when he said that there was no way anybody could have got to her from out here. The balcony of the flat below was too far down as

Kerry lived in the studio apartment right at the top of the building. There was only one possible way to get to her and that was through the door that Blake and Sonia had been standing in front of all night, and neither of them had seen a soul.

Inhaling on his ecig, the same futile thoughts going round his mind, he jumped slightly when the balcony door slid open and there was a deep clearing on a throat behind him. "Blake? Are you alright?"

It was his boss at the station, Inspector Royale. His bushy moustache was quivering more than usual beneath his nose. Blake had often wondered how he coped with it on a day-to-day basis.

"No, not really, Sir," Blake murmured. "I'm confused and I'm angry. Confused as to how the hell this has happened when I was stood outside that apartment all night and angry because I promised her that I was going to protect her."

Royale put a hand on his shoulder. "Get some rest. You've been up all night."

"I haven't got time to rest, Sir!" Blake replied irritably. "I need to find out who did this!"

"And you will. We all will," Royale said calmly. "But you're of no use to me when you're sleep deprived. I want you to go home and get your head down for a few hours. We'll meet you back at the station this evening." He put his hand up as Blake went to interrupt him. "That is an *order*, DS Harte."

When he used his full title like that, Blake knew that there was no point in arguing. He nodded and walked back into the apartment.

As he left the apartment, he was surprised to see Mattison and his girlfriend and colleague, Mini Patil, standing by the door appearing to be having the most discreet argument they could. They both jumped when they realised that Blake was standing behind them.

"Something the matter?" Blake asked.

Patil glanced at Mattison but shook her head. "No, *no*. Nothing, Sir." She was clutching what looked like a leaflet in her hand.

"What's that?"

Mattison looked at the ground and shuffled his feet uncomfortably. "I found it on the coffee table."

"It's a pamphlet from the abortion clinic," Patil added, handing it to Blake. "Kerry lived alone, didn't she?"

Blake raised his eyebrows as he read the contents of the leaflet. "That's right, yes."

"Then it looks like she was pregnant fairly recently." Patil said.

The drive back to Harmschapel did not take long and the roads were still quiet, which was fortunate as by the time Blake pulled up outside Juniper Cottage, his eyes were starting to close.

As he got out the car, the door to the cottage open

and Harrison stepped out, smiling cheerfully when he saw Blake. "Morning! I just tried to ring you."

"My phone's died, sorry."

"I've been called into work," Harrison said, rolling his eyes. "I was going to leave the spare key under the bin or something. How did the new job go?"

Blake was too tired to think properly. "New job?"

"You know, you being a security guard for the night?" Harrison grinned. "Did you eat donuts? That's what they all do, isn't it?"

Blake gave him a weak smile. "I'll explain later."

Harrison nodded. "I'll come 'round when I finish, shall I? I guess we need to start talking about me moving some stuff in." He smiled excitedly. With all that had happened, Blake had completely forgotten about him asking Harrison to move in.

"Yeah," Blake replied, scratching the back of his head. "I don't think I'm going to be around much tonight."

"Oh, okay." Blake could tell he was disappointed. "Something come up?"

"Yeah, you could say that," said Blake. "I'll ring you. I promise."

"No worries. I'll speak to you later." He kissed Blake and walked off down the road, a definite spring in his step.

Blake sighed and he watched Harrison disappear around the corner. He was cursing himself for not telling his boyfriend about what had happened, especially now they were moving forwards. He knew all too well that for their relationship and his work to be compatible, Blake would have to be honest. But he had a thought that was going around his head, an unavoidable truth that Blake knew would worry Harrison, who could be quite an anxious person at the best of times due to events in his own life. But Blake knew that, for the moment, he was better off not knowing. Because for him to have any hope in working out how Kerry Nightingale was killed, Blake was going to have to pay another visit to Thomas Frost.

CHAPTER
EIGHT

Jamie was lying in bed staring up at the ceiling, his clothes from the night before in a crumpled pile on the floor. He thought that the walk home from Clayton Apartments had sobered him up somewhat, but the hangover he had thumping around his body suggested otherwise. He only had extremely vague recollections of what he had done the previous night.

The one thought he remembered having before he had passed out was that the hope that the events of the night would be too blurred for him to remember properly, but the conversation he had had with Kerry was crystal clear and his fury had not diminished.

He had disturbed himself last night with the thoughts of what he had wanted to do to her to make her feel even a small amount of the pain that he felt at this moment. How could she be so heartless as to abort his baby without even telling him, then run away to Spain? Right now, she would be on the plane, probably relieved that she had left him and all other problems behind.

"Cowardly *bitch!*" he shouted, kicking out his foot into a pile of boxes at the end of his bed. They were full of old CDs and DVDs that he had been planning to sell, and as they crashed to the floor, his head throbbed wildly again.

His mobile rang and for the fifth time that day it was Sonia. He had ignored her calls ever since they had woken him up earlier that morning and had been unable to fall asleep again. Like it had all the other times, the ringing stopped followed by a brief pause and another notification that she had left him a voicemail. Jamie had absolutely no intention of speaking to her today. Somebody could have died and she would not hold his attention today.

His bedroom door opened and his housemate, Marcus, poked his head around the door. His tall and lanky frame, scruffily waxed hair, and boyish grin irritated Jamie more than it normally would this morning.

"Alright lad? You trashing your room again?"

"Yep. You never heard of knocking?"

Marcus scoffed and stepped into the room. The smell of his aftershave wafted towards Jamie and it was not an odour that went well with his hangover. "You missed a good night last night mate. I had this bird 'round. Gorgeous, she was. She even brought her mate, and she was *proper* fit. You'd have been in there, bro."
"

"I'm not interested," Jamie replied, turning on his side.

"Ah, come on man," Marcus said, prodding his back. "You've got to get over that Kerry lass. There's nothing she's got that tons of other women out there haven't got. You wanna forget about her."

"That easy, is it?"

"Course it is. You've just gotta move on. Accept that she's not that into you anymore."

The words stung like nettles around Jamie's mind. He sat up and stared at Marcus angrily. "Yeah. You're right. And do you know *how* I know that?"

Marcus looked nervously back at him. "How?"

"She was *pregnant*."

Marcus' eyes widened. "What?"

"*Pregnant*. Emphasis on *was*. I went to see her last night and found a leaflet from the abortion clinic. She was pregnant with my baby and she got rid of it.

That's how I know how little she cared about me. She wasn't even going to tell me. And right now she's sunning herself in Spain, 'cause she's ran away."

Marcus' stunned expression had not faltered. "Pregnant? Are you sure?"

"She told me," Jamie said, slightly more calmly. "I pretty much had to force it out of her."

Marcus stood up and paced around the room. "How far gone was she?"

Before Jamie could reply, there was a loud knock at the front door. After a couple of seconds, the knock came again, louder this time and more frantic.

"Who the hell is that?" Jamie groaned, sinking back into his bed again.

"I'll get it," Marcus said before quickly leaving the room.

Jamie closed his eyes and listened for the conversation at the door. Another surge of frustration flooded through him as he heard Sonia's voice.

"Is Jamie in?" she asked, sounding out of breath. "I really need to speak to him, it's urgent."

"Erm, yeah," he heard Marcus reply, much to his annoyance. "He's in bed – *Oi*, but he's asleep! Don't just –"

But before Marcus could finish, Sonia burst into Jamie's room and was stared down at him, her eyes wide and fearful.

Jamie glared at her. "What do *you* want?"

"Go on then," Sonia said, appearing to be trying to keep her voice steady. "How did you do it? I mean you're clever, I'll give you that."

"*What?*"

"How did you get past us? It doesn't make any sense. I mean, never mind that, but how could you *do* it Jamie?" She was sweating even more than usual and looked like she wanted to either burst into tears or launch herself at him. He sat up and shook his head. "What the *hell* are you on about?"

Behind her, Marcus appeared in the doorway to watch proceedings.

"She's *dead,* Jamie," Sonia snapped. "Dead. And you're the *only* person who could have done it."

There was a deafening silence in the room. Jamie stared at her, unable to comprehend what she was saying. "What? Who's dead? What are you *talking* about?"

"You know who I'm —"

"*Kerry,* Jamie! Kerry is *dead.* Murdered, and you are the only person that hated her *that* much!" Sonia shouted, tearing up and pointing her finger furiously at him.

"Wait, hang on a minute," Marcus interjected from behind her, putting a hand on her shoulder. "He was here all night, I heard him come in!"

"What, at eight o'clock this morning?" Sonia snapped, pushing his hand away. "It *was* you, wasn't it? Why did you do it, Jamie? All because of the baby?"

Jamie was now sat up and staring at her open mouthed, unable to speak.

"Mate?" Marcus murmured, looking at him with horror, before turning back to Sonia. "Look, it can't have been him. I heard his music playing in his room when I got home, he's been here all night!"

"She's dead?" Jamie repeated. He felt absolutely numb. "How can she be dead?"

"Drop the innocent act," Sonia snapped, turning on her heels. "The police will be wanting to speak to you. I'd get your story straight if I were you, because the guy leading the investigation is going to do everything he can to bring the killer to justice."

"Why?" Jamie asked, his voice faint. "What do they know?"

"They've interviewed me, Jamie!" Kerry replied hotly. "'*Can you think of anybody who might want to harm Kerry Nightingale?' 'Oh, well there is the guy who was sleeping with her, whose baby she got rid of without telling him!*'"

Jamie glared at her furiously. "You *told* them that?"

"How could I *lie*?" Sonia shouted back. "Kerry was the nicest woman in the world! There *is* nobody else who could want her dead! You said she was going to pay for what she did, and didn't she just?"

"I think you better go," Marcus said quickly as

Jamie stood up, anger in his eyes.

"Yeah," Jamie said quietly, fury pumping through him. "I think that's a good idea."

"Just know this," Sonia said viciously as she turned to walk out of the room. "If you did do it, there's no way you're going to be able to wiggle your way out of it. I told you that the way you were acting was dangerous!"

"*Get out!*" Jamie yelled. He picked up the nearest thing he could lay his hands on, and threw it across the room. As it left his grip, he realised it was a mug that his father had given him, the last gift he had ever received from him. It smashed against the closing door, with Marcus and Sonia on the other side.

As the anger turned to grief at what he had been told, Jamie sank to his knees, picking up the pieces of the smashed mug and looking at them in his hands. In the past twenty-four hours, he had lost a child he never knew he was supposed to have with a woman who he realised he had fallen head over heels for, more than anyone he had ever met. Through the despair, Sonia's words rang out. The police were looking for him, perhaps going to be here at any moment. He had been so drunk last night, and so angry, and he knew that in his state, some extremely dark thoughts had gone through his head. As he heard Marcus instructing Sonia to leave the house and the front door slamming behind her, Jamie realised that she could be right.

After he had stormed out of the flat, after discovering the abortion leaflet, he had ended up drinking more, meaning everything was a blank. He sat down on the floor and sobbed into his knees, like a small child.

Maybe he had done it.

CHAPTER NINE

Blake's eyes ached with tiredness as he watched his officers take their seats in the briefing room. Despite the fact that he had fallen asleep almost the second his head had hit the pillow, he had awoken feeling just as exhausted as he had when he had arrived home.

"Okay, thank you," he said loudly over the chatter. "Good evening, everybody. Let's get started." He glanced at the empty seat in front of him. Patil, who was in her usual seat in front of him followed his eye line and looked down at her notes uncomfortably.

"Where's Matti?" Blake asked her.

Patil shrugged. "No idea."

Before Blake could question her further, the door was flung open and Mattison strolled in. He looked more irritated than Blake had ever seen him. It was unusual to see the normally happy and keen to please young officer not only out of sorts, but late.

"Sorry, Sir," mumbled Mattison. He threw a brief glance at Patil, but she did not return it.

Pushing the question of what was going on between the two of them, Blake picked up his folder and addressed the room.

"Right, I take it you've all been briefed on what's happened?"

"Yes," drawled Gardiner from the back of the room. "You were standing guard over somebody and yet she still managed to get herself murdered."

Blake exhaled to stop himself biting his sergeant's head off. "Thank you, Michael." He pulled out the picture of Kerry's body from the forensics folder and placed it on the board.

"*Kerry Nightingale*," he began. "Thirty-five years of age. She was found dead this morning at approximately eight AM." He pointed to the wound in the centre of her neck, a pang of guilt hitting him as he did so. "Cause of death, as far as we can tell, was strangulation, with a thin piece of rope or wire. And, as Michael has so kindly pointed out, the murder was somehow committed right under my nose. As I'm sure you're all aware, the door, which myself and one of the security team of the apartment were posted by, was the only way into the flat. Nobody could have gotten in or out with us seeing them. The only other thing that could have possibly been regarded as an escape route was the balcony, the door of which was locked. We found no murder weapon at the scene, or any fingerprints that would indicate that there was anybody else in the flat before we found the body. Everyone with me so far?"

There was a murmuring around the room.

"May we ask something at this point?" Gardiner interjected. "Just why you were standing guard outside this woman's apartment?"

Blake sighed. "Yes." He pulled out the next photograph from the file and placed it on the board. His insides ran cold as the face on the photo glowered back at him. "Thomas Frost. Does the name ring a bell with anybody?"

When there was no answer, Inspector Royale, who was standing in the doorway of his office, watching proceedings, cleared his throat. "Serial killer from a few years back. Went by the name of Jack Frost according to the media."

A slight mumbling of recognition rippled around the room.

"DS Harte was the officer who arrested him,"

Royale added.

"Well, it wasn't just me, but yes. Frost was the case that earned me my detective rank, as a matter of fact," Blake said. He reached into the file and pulled out another set of photographs, placing them each on the board, one at a time. "Julie Carlisle, Donna Atkins, Leanne Egan, Grace Hodgekiss, and Suzanne Meyer. All victims of Frost." The names were labelled underneath each photograph of the women but Blake did not need them. He remembered each name and each murder vividly.

"I remember now," Patil said quietly. "'*Frostbitten*' I think the papers went for after his arrest?"

Blake rolled his eyes and nodded.

"Commendable as it was for you to bring that nutcase to justice," Gardiner asked, an air of derision in his voice, "What does any of that have to do with Kerry Nightingale?"

"Believe it or not Michael, that's an excellent question," Blake told him. "When we arrested Thomas Frost, he was just about to claim Kerry as his sixth victim. We burst in to her house, where he had been waiting for her, just as he was about to kill her. He had her on the floor and was in the process of throttling her with a piece of rope."

"The same way she was killed last night?" Mattison clarified.

Blake nodded. "And, last night's death was a

similar, if not identical MO to his other victims." He indicated the lines around the previous victim's necks on their pathology photographs and then to Kerry's, before taking a deep breath. He was not sure how well what he was going to say next would be received. "A few days ago, I went to visit Thomas Frost in prison."

There was a brief silence before Gardiner piped up. "What on earth for?"

"Because he asked to see me," Blake replied, trying not to look Royale in the eye. "And, ever since his arrest, he's never stopped talking about Kerry. But this time, he made a threat. He said she'd been dead by the end of the week, and here we are investigating her murder."

"Hang on a minute," Gardiner said, closing his eyes in confusion. "You're saying that this man is still locked up, under constant observation?"

"Yes."

"With no way of getting out of his prison?"

"Correct."

"So, in what possible capacity could he be responsible?"

"That," replied Blake, "is what we are going to find out tomorrow."

"You're planning on going back to interview Frost?" Royale clarified from the doorway. "In the prison?"

"I don't see how I've got much choice, Sir," Blake

replied. "He might be locked up, but he still threatened a murder that ended up coming to pass. A murder he's been *promising* for seven years. I've got to speak to him again."

Royale sighed. "I don't like it, Blake. This man is dangerous. He's surely just going to try and play games with you. What incentive has he got to help you? He's already in prison, what more could be done to him?"

Blake scratched the back of his head and nodded. "I know. But I've got to try. I know Frost, I know how his mind works. Trust me, Sir, if I can, I will get something out of him."

The next morning, Blake pulled up outside the prison and stared at the entrance gates. Royale's doubts about just how helpful the interview was going to be had been bothering him ever since the meeting, despite the fact that he had been mentally rehearsing his question as well as how he was going to ask them ever since.

He glanced across to Mattison who was also looking at the gates with an air of trepidation. "Last chance, Matti," he said. "I won't think any less of you if you don't want to do this. He's a dangerous man."

Mattison turned to look at Blake resolutely. "I'm a police officer, Sir," he replied. "It's my job. Besides, if I'm being perfectly honest, I'm kind of curious. I've never met a serial killer before."

"He's not a celebrity, Matti," Blake said seriously.

"This man strangled five women to death, and in some way is responsible for a sixth death. He's evil. And he prays on weakness and vulnerability."

"I'm hardly vulnerable, Sir," Mattison replied indignantly.

"No, sorry, I mean, he'll be able to sense your inexperience and he's going to try and play with that. Unless you follow what I've told you to do."

"I promise you, Sir, I know exactly what you've told me."

"Tell me again," Blake said.

"I'm to be cold and unresponsive. Ideally don't say anything to him at all. I'm there purely as an extra authority. Don't humour him, don't entertain him."

Blake sighed. Given the choice, he would never have considered an officer of Mattison's experience anywhere near Frost, but he had been the only one available. "Okay," he replied. "Let's go in.

Unlike the last time Blake and Frost had met, this time they were in a visiting room. When they walked in, Frost was sitting behind a large pane of glass, so that there was no way he could try anything with either Blake or Mattison.

As before, a prison guard followed them into the room and locked the door. Blake watched Frost as they approached the glass and sat down opposite him. Frost's eyes were immediately on Mattison, and Blake did not like it. Even without saying anything, Mattison was naturally young looking with his smooth face and lightly gelled hair.

"Good morning," Frost said, his voice as smooth as ever. "I rather thought I'd be seeing you again, Mr Harte."

Blake said nothing.

"And who's this you've brought to see me?" Frost said icily, staring at Mattison. "Is it bring your child to work day?"

As instructed, Mattison didn't reply. Blake turned his head to the prison guard. "Are we recording?" The guard nodded. "Interview commencing at nine forty six. Present in the interview is myself, Detective Sergeant Blake Harte, Police Constable Billy Mattison, Andrew Dixon, a guard at the prison, and Thomas Frost."

"Billy?" Frost said, ignoring Blake's preamble and staring at Mattison with a smirk. "What a *mature* sounding name. Is it your first day?"

"*Oi*," Blake said sharply, clicking his fingers. "Eyes on me."

Frost smirked at Blake. "Oh you have my *full* attention, Detective, I assure you."

"I'd like to start with asking you about Kerry Nightingale." Blake began.

"Kerry?" Frost said innocently. "I don't think I know a Kerry."

"Is that a fact?" Blake said, producing a photograph. It was an ordinary picture of Kerry, as opposed to the forensic snap of her body. Blake knew how much of a kick Frost would get out of seeing that. "So, you've forgotten about the woman you attempted to murder seven years ago, then?"

"I murdered a lot of women, Detective," Frost chuckled, glancing at Mattison. "Did he tell you about my murders, Billy? Little bit above you, I should think. You won't have met anybody like me before, will you?"

Again, Mattison did not reply. Blake was pleased to see that his deadpan expression had not altered since he had entered the room.

"A few days ago, you made a threat," Blake continued, holding up the photograph. "You said that Kerry Nightingale would be dead within the week."

"*Did* I?" Frost said, looking surprised. "Are you *sure?*"

Blake frowned for a second, as he tried to work out what Frost was playing at. He had been expecting him to be gloating, to be revelling in the fact that he was being interviewed about a murder he had dreamt of since the door on his cell had first been locked.

"Tell me, Billy," Frost said. "Do you know what your colleague is referring to? Or are you a bit young to be given details like that?"

"Stop talking to him, I'm the one you're here to

talk to," Blake snapped at him. "Tell me about Kerry."

"But I told you," Frost replied, looking at Blake with almost serene confusion. "I don't know what threats you're referring to. Could you produce any proof of these threats?"

"Proof?" Blake repeated, slightly taken aback.

"This interview, I mean the one you're doing now," Frost said, leaning back in his chair. "It's being recorded, isn't it? I mean this is one of your official little chats that you police do from time to time?"

Blake closed his eyes, cursing his own stupidity. He knew what Frost was getting at before he had even said it.

"I mean, if you and I have had a previous conversation, I expect you've got a recording of that to refer back to?" Frost asked him lightly.

Blake leant forwards. "Listen, I *know* you were involved in this somehow. You *know* what I'm talking about, and you *know* how it happened and who did it. We'll be going through the records of anybody who has visited you, searching your cell. You thought you had no privacy in here now? You've seen nothing yet."

"The only person who ever visits me is Simon, Detective. He likes to keep himself to himself though, so you might have some trouble finding him."

"Who's Simon?" Blake asked him.

"My son. Do you have children, Billy? Have you even been to bed with a girl, yet?"

"When did you last see him?" Blake inquired.

Frost ignored him, he was still examining Mattison. "No, I don't suppose you have. You're just a little boy, really, aren't you?"

"You were asked a question, so answer it," Mattison suddenly snapped. "When did you last see your son?"

Blake frowned and threw him a look. Mattison bit his lip.

Frost looked delighted. "Oh, toys are out the pram! You've never been one for travelling without a colleague with a big mouth, Mr Harte. What was the name of your other one? Sally something? I didn't like her. She didn't have much up top." He glanced at Mattison. "Still though, at least she was old enough to vote."

"Take him back to his cell," Blake told the guard. "I'll find out what we need to know myself. Interview terminated at nine fifty-one AM."

He stood up and the guard opened the door to let him out. Frost smiled cheerfully behind the glass. "Going so soon? But we were just getting acquainted, Billy!"

As Blake followed Mattison out of the room, the sound of Frost's mocking laughter rang in his ears. Once the door had been closed, Blake turned to Mattison as he leant against the wall with his face in his hands.

"I'm sorry, Sir," he said quietly.

"You were dealing with him admirably, Matti. What happened?"

Mattison shook his head. "He just wound me up, telling me how young and immature I looked. Bloody creep." He kicked the wall he was leaning against, with an air of frustration.

"And I told you that was what he would do," Blake replied, looking at him with concern. "You let him get to you, that's how he works in those sorts of situations."

Mattison rubbed his eyes and sighed. "Sorry, Sir. Look, is it alright if I wait for you in the car?"

Blake nodded. Without another word, Mattison sighed again and disappeared down the corridor. Blake watched him leave, his eyes narrowed, wondering if his strange mood had anything to do with the apparent fall out with Patil.

Mentally putting a pin in the matter, he turned to the guard. "I need access to Frost's visitor records, any post he's had, anything that comes under the category of communication with the outside world."

The guard nodded. "He gets mail, but it's all vetted. Most of it is from those weird people who seem to have a fetish for the insane, you know how it is."

Blake nodded and rolled his eyes. He never understood the fascination that people had with someone like Frost, especially from women; but they existed. Women with an overwhelming sense of loneliness in their lives exuding it into somebody they perceived to be raw and exciting. People like Frost would get fan mail, almost as much as somebody on television.

Walking into the prison guard's office, he was greeted by a group of the other guards crowded around a television screen. One of them, an older woman, turned to Blake as he entered.

"You the one who's been investigating this murder?"

Blake raised an eyebrow. "Yes, why?"

"And you think it's got summit to do with Frost?"

Blake frowned. "I'm investigating all possibilities, why?"

The woman nodded at the screen. "We've got this footage of Frost in his cell from this morning. He started a fight last week so we put him in solitary and those cells have cameras in."

"Okay," Blake said, wondering where this was going. He looked at the screen. It showed Frost lying in his cell bed.

"I know he's just lying there, but he starts acting a bit weird, so we thought it might be of some sort of use to you. He's a nutcase, we know that, so I dunno if it's helpful."

Blake nodded as the woman rewound the footage and clicked play.

The footage showed Frost not moving from his bed, he was just lying there. Blake was just about to ask what he was supposed to be looking at when the footage showed Frost raising his arms up in front of him and slowly wrapping his hands around something, presumably imaginary in front of him. His fingers closed together, in a throttling motion, a dark smile appearing on his face.

Blake stared at the screen. "Has he ever done that before?"

"Not that we've ever seen," replied the guard.

"And this was this morning?"

"Yeah, when we wake them up. Eight o'clock this morning."

Blake's heart skipped a beat. The time in the corner of the screen confirmed what the guard was saying. It read eight AM, the exact time of the murder.

When Blake returned to the car, he found Mattison sitting in the passenger seat, staring up at the ceiling.

"So," Blake said to him as he climbed in. "Are you going to tell me what's wrong, or am I going to have to drag it out of you?"

Mattison shuffled uncomfortably in his seat. "It's honestly nothing, Sir. I'm just being stupid."

Blake raised a disdainful eyebrow. "Is that a fact? So stupid that you let a few jibes from Frost get to you like that? Put it like this, Matti. That could have gone very wrong in there. Frost prays on weakness in people. So we can either go for the formal route, where you don't tell me anything and I always have second thoughts about you ever being a second officer for me in an interview because I don't feel you have the temperament for it, or I can be the nice, understanding DS Harte, and you tell me what's wrong, and we put this down as a blip. Then I try and help you because I know you're a much better officer than the one I just saw in there. Your choice."

Mattison sighed and fiddled with a loose bit of cotton on his trousers. "It's Mini. Don't tell her I told you this, but –"

He was interrupted by Blake's phone ringing. It was Sharon from forensics. Blake groaned and glanced at Mattison.

"Don't think you're getting off that easily," Blake said, winking at him, before answering the phone. "Hi, Sharon."

"Blake, I've emailed you the pathology report on Kerry Nightingale, but there was something that I figured you'd want to know sooner rather than later." Sharon said, in her usual sharp tone of voice. Blake could always imagine her rushing down a corridor to her next task whenever they spoke in circumstances like this.

"Go on," he said.

"That leaflet from the abortion clinic that we found in her flat," Sharon continued. "Turns out we may have jumped the gun ever so slightly."

"What do you mean?"

"Because she hasn't *had* an abortion. She was pregnant. About six weeks gone, I'd say."

Blake raised his eyebrows and exhaled. "Wow. She kept that one quiet, then."

"Apart from that, I didn't find anything out of the ordinary. Cause of death was strangulation with a thin piece of rope or wire."

"Okay, thanks for letting me know," Blake said. He ended the call and exhaled, his brain whirring.

"What's happened?" Mattison asked him.

"Turns out Kerry *was* still pregnant. That abortion leaflet must have been something she was thinking about, rather than something she'd already had done."

Mattison scratched the back of his head. "And her ex-lover, Jamie, according to a witness statement, stormed out of her flat last night, telling Kerry she would pay for getting rid of his baby?"

Blake nodded. "Jamie Salford. I think it's time we paid him a visit."

CHAPTER
TEN

Jamie sat on the floor of the shower, the water raining down on him, with the steam rising up from his body, misting up the glass. The water had gotten steadily hotter the longer he had been in there, but he had barely noticed. His mind felt like a DVD that was skipping; all he could see was Sonia saying *'She's dead, Jamie. Kerry is dead,'* over and over again. As the water began to run into his eyes, he closed them and tried to remember where he had gone and what he had done after leaving Kerry's apartment the night before, but try as he might, it was all a blur.

He knew that the bruise on his arm was from fighting with someone he had had a disagreement with in the club he had started the night in, and that was what worried him more than anything. When he had arrived at Kerry's apartment, he had already been angry and was feeling violent; who was to say whether Kerry had ended up on the receiving end of it?

A loud knocking on the bathroom door broke into his thoughts.

"Dude," Marcus called through the bathroom door. "There's two policemen here to see you."

Jamie sighed, his stomach performing a somersault. This is the moment he had been dreading. If even Sonia suspected him of killing Kerry, what were the police going to think?

He pulled himself up and turned off the water, grabbed a towel and tied it around his waist, trying to think of something to say to the officers that would abscond him in some way from the events.

He walked out onto the landing. As he walked past the top of the stairs, he saw Blake waiting at the bottom.

"Afternoon, Jamie," Blake said, nodding curtly. "Quick as you like, please. We need a word."

"I won't be long, I'll just get some clothes on," Jamie replied, trying to judge from Blake's tone just how much trouble he was in.

"Don't be long, please," Blake replied, smiling

cheerfully at him. He turned on his heels and walked into the living room, leaving Jamie at the top of the stairs, feeling more worried and defensive than ever.

By the time that Jamie walked into the living room, Marcus was sitting on the edge of the sofa looking nervily at Blake, who was sat sipping a mug of tea, with another officer sitting next to him. They all looked up as Jamie entered.

"Ah, there you are," Blake said, placing the mug on the floor. "I don't think we've been properly introduced, Jamie. Detective Sergeant Harte, this is my colleague, PC Mattison. We'd like to speak to you about the death of Kerry Nightingale."

"I don't know anything," Jamie said hurriedly.

Blake nodded. "In that case, this shouldn't take very long. Would you mind, Marcus?"

Marcus practically jumped at the mention of his name and nodded, looking relieved that he was no longer required. He exchanged a worried look with Jamie as he almost ran out of the living room and closed the door behind him without a word.

"Now, then," Blake said. "Do take a seat, Jamie."

Jamie sat in the seat recently vacated by his housemate, but remained silent.

"We wanted to talk to you about your movements last night," Blake told him. "We've had a couple of people tell us that you were a bit drunk last night."

Jamie shrugged. "Not a crime, is it?"

"If it was, we'd have some rather full prisons, wouldn't we?" Blake said cheerfully. "No, the only reason I ask is that we have a witness telling us that you turned up at Kerry's apartment last night, quite worse for wear and you were quite angry."

Jamie struggled for the right words, desperately trying to think of some way to defend himself, so he just nodded.

"What were you so angry about?" Mattison asked him.

"Bare in mind, we do know about your relationship with Kerry," Blake added.

Jamie bit his lip in thought. "I *was* going out with her, yeah. I wasn't anymore, though, she ended things with me."

"And that's why you were so angry?"

"One of the reasons, yeah."

"What else was happening?"

Jamie sighed, running his hands through his hair. "Turns out she was pregnant. I was going to be a dad. She didn't even think it was worth mentioning to me, before she ran off to Spain. She went and had an abortion and if I hadn't have gone there last night, I never would have known."

Blake glanced at Mattison and tilted his head slightly in what looked, to Jamie, like an attempt at sympathy. "We've had the report back from pathologist. Kerry was pregnant when she died."

Jamie's heart seemed to skip a few beats. "What? You mean she hadn't had an abortion?"

Blake shook his head. "Nope. Does that change how you were feeling about her?"

Jamie leant forward and put his head in his hands. It did change how he was feeling, but he found it impossible to describe exactly how his perception of Kerry had altered. So, if the abortion had not happened, what had been her plan? To have the baby in Spain, and just never tell him?

"Did you want to have a baby?" Mattison asked him. "I mean, was it planned?"

Jamie looked up at him, frowning. It seemed like quite a stupid question to him. "Of course it wasn't planned, but I would have been there for it. What would you have expected me to do? Send her a tenner every month for maintenance?"

Blake glanced between the two of them. "Jamie, would you be able to tell me what your movements were last night?"

Jamie shuffled in his seat uncomfortably as the questions he had been dreading arrived. "I'd been out to the club in Clackton – *Eclipse*. I ended up getting pretty drunk."

"Yes, we know that," Blake said. "You turned up to Clayton Apartments, according to one witness, '*off your head.*'"

Jamie scoffed. "You can cut all the '*one witness*' crap, I know it was Sonia that you've spoken too. She couldn't wait for things to go wrong with me and Kerry."

"Do you remember what you said to Kerry?" Blake asked him. "Baring in mind, we do have a witness who was there for quite a lot of the conversation?"

Jamie shrugged. "Not really. I was pretty hammered. The whole reason I'd got that drunk was because I wanted to forget about Kerry."

"But Kerry's apartment was the first place you went to?" Mattison put in lightly.

Jamie glared at him. "What? You never had a falling out with your missus, mate?" He was pleased to see that Mattison looked down at the floor, apparently embarrassed. "I wanted to see if I could patch things up with her. I didn't know about the baby, though I'm guessing that's why she broke up with me."

"Apparently your last words before storming out," Blake said, glancing down at his note pad, "were '*you're scum, you will pay for this.*'" He looked up at Jamie, appearing almost apologetic. "Not exactly helpful last words to a murder victim a few hours before her death, are they?"

"I don't remember saying that," Jamie mumbled. It was perfectly true, his mind was a blank after he had found out about the baby, but he doubted Blake believed him. "But I didn't do anything. I was angry, I must have come straight home after that."

"'*Must have*?'" repeated Blake.

Jamie nodded, shuffling in his seat again. "I don't remember."

Blake scratched the back of his head and looked across at Mattison. "You don't remember where you were, a few hours after your last words to a woman who was later murdered were '*you will pay for this?*' That doesn't exactly constitute as much of an alibi, Jamie."

Jamie's brain whirred, trying to think of something to defend himself with. "Did you ask Marcus, my housemate? I woke up here, in my bed. Did you ask him whether he heard me coming in?"

"We did," Mattison said, nodding. "He says the only thing he heard was the sound of you kicking something in your room at about eleven this morning."

Jamie stood up, pointing at them both defensively. "You can't stich me up for this. I know you're not allowed to charge me without any proof."

"Sit down," Blake told him. "Calm down. We're not accusing you of anything, yet. We're just trying to ascertain your movements. What I would suggest is that you have a good think, because we're going to need to know where you were last night and what you were doing."

"I'm not the first bloke to forget what they did

when they got too drunk," Jamie told them as Blake and Mattison stood up. "You won't be able to pin anything on me. I didn't do it."

"And if that's true, then you're absolutely right," Blake said lightly. "We can't prove you did something that you didn't. But, what I will say, is that if you *did* do it, we will find out. So, I'd get your movements remembered if I was you."

Somehow, even though they were leaving, Jamie felt more nervous than ever.

"If you remember anything, you can get me at Harmschapel police station," Blake said to him, his expression serious. "Don't go on any trips anywhere. We'll be speaking again, very soon. We'll see ourselves out."

Jamie watched them both leave, running his hands through his hair again as he heard the front door close. A few moments later, Marcus poked his head into the room.

"They gone?"

"Why couldn't you have said that you heard me come back last night?" Jamie snapped at him. "I haven't got an alibi! They *think* I did it!"

Marcus' eyes widened. "I can say I've remembered that I heard you? Would that work?"

"Not when you've already told them that you didn't, you tool," Jamie replied irritably. He sat down on the sofa, trying to formulate some sort of plan, but nothing came to mind. "I'm screwed," he murmured. "Kerry's been murdered and as far as they're concerned, I'm the only one who could have done it. What the *hell* am I going to do?"

CHAPTER ELEVEN

When Blake finally arrived home that evening, he was delighted to find Harrison waiting for him on the sofa.

"You have no idea how happy I am to see you," he told him, pulling him in as tightly as he could.

"Likewise," Harrison said, smiling as they both cuddled up together. It was a feeling Blake was happy to get used to. "But is it alright for me to be here tonight? I can't believe what you're dealing with at work at the minute."

"Listen to me," Blake told him, putting a finger on Harrison's lips and winking playfully. "When I get home after a day like today, the only thing I want is for you to be here to hear about how awful my day was, how crap my life is and how I have the worst job on earth."

"You don't believe either of those things," Harrison grinned. "You love your job, and I like to think that your life has improved quite a lot since you moved to Harmschapel?"

Blake nodded and kissed him. "Damn right it has. I know, I just like to be dramatic sometimes. Do you realise how boring it is doing that to an empty room? So yes, I am sure that I want you here tonight and every night afterwards. Clear?"

Harrison grinned again. "Clear."

"Good." He was just about to pull Harrison in for a kiss again when there was a loud ringing from his laptop. There was only one person who could make his laptop make that noise.

"It's Sally," Blake said. "I've got to take this, I need to ask her a few things. Just make yourself at home. Because that is exactly what this place is now, okay?"

"Happy to," Harrison replied, snuggling himself down into the sofa. "Betty will be pleased too."

Blake's heart sank slightly at the mention of Harrison's goat, but he laughed as he walked across the room to the laptop where Sally's Skype call was ringing from.

"Sally-Ann Matthews, you have no idea how happy I am to see your face," Blake said as he connected the call.

Sally's expression at the use of her full name was there as Blake had hoped it would be, but she still smiled. "Likewise. How's it going?"

Blake sighed as he sat down at his computer chair. "How long have you got? You will not believe the day I have had."

And so Blake told Sally all about what had happened. How Thomas Frost had repeatedly asked to speak to him, how he had promised that Kerry would be dead in a few days, the threatening note left on his front door and how, ultimately and impossibly, Kerry had been strangled to death under Blake's supervision.

By the time he was finished, Sally's mouth was wide open. "*Wow.* Thomas Frost? There's a name I hoped would never see the light of day again."

"Tell me about it," Blake said, pulling his ecig out of his pocket and inhaling deeply on it. On the screen, Sally lit one of her usual Lambert and Butler, making Blake want to reach through the screen and grab one out of her packet. "He's lost none of his charm. He even remembers you."

Sally's eyes widened. "Tell him I've been missing for five years and the last you heard I was somewhere in Timbuktu. I've never known a man give me the creeps as much as him. Still, you've got to think logically here, Blake. There's no way he could have got to Kerry. He's in prison. You know how much of a psycho he is. Somehow, he's arranged for one of his criminal underworld friends to kill her."

"Yeah? And how did they do it in a locked apartment that they couldn't have escaped from?"

"By hiding in the lampshade? How should I know? That's your department, Detective. Don't let Frost have as much influence over your thinking in this as I'm guessing he already has. He'd love to know he's still calling the shots, even from his prison cell. My advice would be to remove him the equation entirely for now, and work out how one of his mates managed to get in and out of that apartment without being seen."

Blake nodded. For the first time since this case had begun, it felt like somebody was finally talking some sense to him. "Do you remember anything about Frost's son?"

Sally stubbed out her cigarette and pulled a face. "Not that much. I never met him. I want to say he was called Simon? I can't remember whether that was his actual name or his assumed name after his murderous scum of a father was locked away."

"Assumed name?"

Sally nodded. "Yeah, from what I remember, he

changed his name and location a few weeks after Frost's prison sentence went public."

"Great." Blake sighed. "So he could be absolutely anywhere now, couldn't he? Even with you in Timbuktu."

"Yeah, I guess so." Sally shrugged. "Why do you want to know?"

"He's the only visitor Frost has had in prison," Blake replied. "I was hoping he'd be able to shed some form of light on how he's been able to get in contact with the outside world. He knew what was going to happen, Sal. Right down to what time the murder would be taking place. This has all come from his evil little mind, and I just don't know how he's done it. How did he mastermind this from his prison cell? It just doesn't make any sense."

"I'll try and find out what I can about the son from this end," Sally replied. "I don't know how much good it'll do you though. You know what the relatives are like if they know somebody inside. If they want to be hidden, then they tend to stay hidden."

"Thanks," Blake said. "Anyway, I better go. I've got someone moving in over the next few days." He smiled, without even meaning to. Sally squealed and clapped her hands together.

"Harrison? Oh, Blake. I'm so happy for you. Finally, it's about time you took the next step. Who asked who?"

"I asked him, of course," Blake replied. "It's great, Sal. If anything, just to see how much his confidence has grown. It's like he's a completely different bloke to the one I met cowering in his abusive boyfriend's shadow. The only thing I've got to worry about is that bloody goat of his. Sally, it hates me. It only has to lay eyes on me and it's got murder in its eyes. I swear to God," he said over Sally's laughter. "It wants me dead!"

Sally lit another cigarette. "Two seconds on Google would throw you up some great recipes for a goat curry?"

Blake laughed. "*Sssh*! Last thing I want is Harrison thinking I've got it in for his pet. He loves that thing."

"I shouldn't worry," Sally told him, putting her hands in her blouse and fidgeting. A few seconds later, she had a bra in her hand and sighed with relief. "It'll be dead soon. Goats don't live that long, do they? I'll leave you to it. Love you!"

"Love you too," Blake told her.

As Sally's face disappeared from the screen, he leant back in his chair and sighed. Whatever else might have been going on, Blake could hardly deny that he was extremely lucky.

A bottle of beer attached to a hand appeared over the top of his shoulder. "Fancy watching a film?"

Blake nodded. "That is exactly what I fancy. How did you know?"

"Good," Harrison smiled. "And while we're deciding which one, you can tell me what Sally meant when she was on about goat curry?"

CHAPTER
TWELVE

Jamie downed the shot of vodka and slammed the glass down on the bar, indicating to the barman that he wanted another. The man behind the bar raised an eyebrow, but poured him another without a word.

Jamie could feel the judgemental eyes on him from all angles, but he was far beyond caring. All he wanted to do was forget everything that had happened to him in the past week. With each shot he drank, he imagined a section of his memories of Kerry disintegrating, then he became more annoyed with himself when her face remained at the forefront of his mind.

He gagged slightly as the neat vodka hit the back of his throat, but he resolutely repeated the process of wordlessly demanding another, pulling his wallet out of his pocket and passing the barman a twenty pound note. As the newest shot began to take effect, he looked around the bar. The only thing on his mind now was to pull someone. He wanted meaningless, stress relieving sex, and perhaps in the process, mess with the girl's head as much as Kerry had messed with his.

As his drunken eyes scanned the bar, he spotted a young woman walk into the bar. She had caramel covered skin, short black hair cascading down her shoulders, and gave the impression of someone delicate, impressionable, and naïve. With the mind-set of a cheetah stalking a deer in the long grass, Jamie watched her walk across the dance floor and towards the bar, exhaling, perhaps with stress, when she arrived. He sidled over to her as she pulled her purse out of her handbag and attracted the barman's attention.

"I'll get that if you like," Jamie offered.

The woman glanced at him, raising an eyebrow. "You can if you like, it won't get you anywhere though."

Jamie shrugged and passed the barman another

note out of his wallet, ordering another vodka for himself in the process.

The woman thanked him all the same and when the drinks arrived, she took a large gulp of it.

"Tough day?" Jamie asked her, sipping his vodka.

The woman rolled her eyes. "You could say that."

"Must have been if you're here on your own," Jamie replied, indicating the bar.

"So are you," noted the woman. "Looks like that is far from your first."

Jamie shrugged again. "Maybe we were meant to help each other through a tough day. Talking to a complete stranger, I'm told it helps."

The woman looked at him with amusement. "So, this isn't you trying to chat me up, this is just you being a good Samaritan, is that what you're telling me?"

Jamie nodded. "Tell Uncle Jamie your problems."

The woman laughed. "Nothing you can sort out, trust me. I just had an argument with my boyfriend."

The mention of a boyfriend did nothing to deter Jamie's intentions. "That's a shame. Serious row?"

"We just need to sit and talk," she replied. "Nothing that a bit of communication won't fix." She took another large swig of her drink. "I hope. So, go on then. What about you? No girlfriend?"

Jamie downed the rest of his vodka, debating how to answer. "No, not really," he replied. "I'm not really boyfriend material. I'm more your go-to guy when you want to forget about your problems." He leant across the bar and brushed her hand with his finger. "So if you want to forget about that argument with your fella, just say the word. What did you say your name was again?"

She recoiled and moved her hand away from him and was just about to reply when there was a loud shout from the entrance to the bar.

"*Mini!*"

Jamie's teeth gritted when he realised who it was glaring at them from across the bar. Mattison, the officer who had interviewed him with Blake stormed across the dance floor and stared at them, an accusing fury in his eyes.

"What the hell, Mini?" Mattison snapped, gesturing at Jamie. "You storm off and I find you here, chatting up someone we're supposed to be investigating?"

Patil gasped and stared at Jamie.

Jamie smirked at Mattison. "Yeah. You didn't mention that your boyfriend was a copper. Especially not *this* one."

"This is Jamie Salford," Mattison told her, glaring at Jamie with intense dislike. "The guy me and Harte were interviewing today?"

Patil pushed her drink aside. "Trust me, Matti. I wasn't chatting him up. It was more the other way, I *promise."*

Jamie scoffed. "Still let me buy you a drink though, didn't you darling?"

"Can we go?" Mattison snapped. "Or would you rather stay and completely mess up the case?"

Patil grabbed her handbag off the bar. "I'm going, so quit the attitude."

"Sounds like you're compensating for something, mate. Little man syndrome, is it?" Jamie said slyly. "Can't keep your missus happy at home, so she comes looking elsewhere?"

In the three seconds it took for Mattison to step towards Jamie, Patil had already thrown herself between them and was pushing Mattison towards the exit. "*Move,*" she ordered.

"See you soon, Mini!" Jamie called as Mattison was frogmarched out of the bar. "Bet you look even better in uniform!"

He chuckled to himself as he turned back towards the bar again. The exchange had made him feel better, but now she was gone he was stuck with nobody to distract him from his problems again. He caught the attention of a barman he knew and waved his empty glass at him.

"Don't you think you've had enough, Jamie?" the barman said, glancing at the door where Patil and Mattison had just walked through. "I don't want you causing any more trouble."

"I'll decide when I've had enough. I've got stuff going on and the last thing I need is a lecture, so just do your job, Matt, yeah?"

Matt leant across the bar. "I heard about Kerry, I'm sorry, mate. I know the two of you were close."

Jamie grunted in reply. The last thing he wanted from anybody was sympathy.

"I saw her in town only a few weeks ago. Crazy to think what's happened since." Matt said, picking up a row of glasses from the bar. "I don't know who she was with, some tall bloke walking her back to those apartments. It's where she lived, wasn't it?"

Jamie had not really been listening to what he was saying, but his attention had been caught by the mention of another man. "Tall bloke?"

"Yeah," Matt said, gesturing with his arms. "'Bout six foot, I'd say. Dark brown hair, had one of those tank tops on. They went inside together, I don't know who he was, I couldn't quite make him out."

Jamie's eyes narrowed. "What night was this?"

Matt shrugged. "Six weeks ago? Tuesday it was, I was on my way to help close. Yeah, he was a tall bloke. I assume you two had moved on since then, cause they looked pretty close."

There was only one man he knew who fitted that description, but he was having difficulty believing it could be him. Without another word, he stormed out of the bar and began walking towards Clayton

Apartments.

"What are *you* doing here?" Sonia said to him as Jamie stormed through the door. He ignored her, punched the combination into the keypad on the reception door, and strode straight towards the cameras.

Sonia watched him, her eyes wide over the top of her crime book as he tapped angrily on the keyboard to bring up the footage that he needed to see. The one person who had listened to him lament about Kerry, his only true friend through the heartache he felt he had been subject to, surely he wouldn't do something like this.

The footage began to load up, and now Jamie was watching the corridor of Kerry's apartment, as he had so much the past couple of weeks. He clicked fast forward on the computer, his heart racing, waiting for her to come into view.

"Jamie, what the hell are you doing?" Sonia said sharply. "Haven't you done enough –"

"*Shut it*," Jamie snapped at her as on the screen, the lift doors on the top floor opened and Kerry stepped out. Briefly, Jamie's heart ached as he saw her smiling, laughing at the person behind her in the lift. And then he appeared. All six foot of him, his unmistakable lanky stature – Marcus.

Kerry leant up to put her arms around his neck and pulled him in for a long, lingering kiss. Beside him, Sonia gasped, but Jamie could barely hear her. As he watched Kerry bite her bottom lip in the same seductive fashion she always used to do with him, she took his hand and led him into her flat, the door closing behind them.

"Jamie, I don't know what to say," Sonia murmured.

"It was *him*." Jamie said quietly. "That's why she never told me about the baby. That's why he looked so shocked when I told him. It wasn't even mine. It was *his*."

Sonia shook her head in disbelief. "How could he do that? He knew how crazy you were about her."

Jamie sunk into the chair in front of the desk, furious and dazed. "That's why she broke up with me. Because she was seeing him. Then all of a sudden she's pregnant." He slammed his fist down on the desk, causing Sonia to jump. "I *knew* it. We were always so careful. We always used protection."

Sonia put her hand on his shoulder. "Don't do anything stupid, Jamie. You're already in enough trouble."

"Oh, I haven't even started yet," Jamie whispered, his eyes returning to the screen and to the now empty flat corridor, the footage continuing to roll, with only a door blocking the camera's view of what was happening behind it. He stood up and threw the reception door open, and stormed out of the building, barely hearing Sonia shouting his name.

CHAPTER THIRTEEN

Having spent most of the night tossing and turning with the sparse details he had managed to accumulate of the case spinning around his head, Blake arrived at work the next morning feeling like he had hardly slept at all. The stroll to the station had been slower than usual. He had wanted to arrive at work with some solid theories about what had happened, how Kerry had been killed, whether it was possible for Jamie Salford to have done it, as well as how what would otherwise could be a domestic argument gone horribly wrong could in any way be connected to Thomas Frost. Although he was still waiting for Sally to find out what she could about Frost's son, Simon, Blake was not even sure whether it would be of any help to him.

Vaguely nodding at the messages that Mandy Darnwood, the sergeant on the desk that day, gave him as he passed on his way to the meeting room, Blake's mind went back to the discovery of Kerry on the floor of her bedroom, frantically trying to work out if there was something blindingly obvious he had missed. The bedroom had been fairly dark when Blake had walked in, before Sonia had pulled open the curtains. Was there something he could have missed in the dark?

Already feeling mentally exhausted, he pushed open the doors and was surprised to find Patil alone in the room, already sat at the table, staring into space.

"Morning, Mini," Blake said, pulling off his coat. "You're here early, aren't you?"

Patil looked up at him. "I came in early."

Blake sat down opposite her. "Should I be commending your commitment or asking what's wrong?"

Patil tried to smile, but instead her bottom lip quivered and she burst into tears. Blake nodded and put an arm around her.

"Okay," he said. "Come on. It's alright. Tell me. Tell me what's happened."

It took a few moments for Patil to calm herself

down enough to reply. "It's Billy."

Again, Blake nodded. "What's Matti done?"

"He hasn't done anything, that's the thing," Patil sniffled. "It's all me. I've just completely wrecked things."

"How?" Blake said, glancing at the clock. He hoped he would be able to calm her down before the rest of the team arrived.

Patil sighed. "I don't even know where to begin." She wiped her eyes and took the tissue that Blake had offered her from his pocket. "I've known that man most of my life, Sir. We both grew up here, we joined the force together. I love him. I honestly love the bones of him."

"So?" Blake asked softly. "What's the problem?"

"He wants us to start a family," Patil sobbed. "Me and him. *A baby.*"

Blake raised his eyebrows in surprise. For the time he had known Mattison, he had never perceived him as a particularly paternal type person. "Matti? Really?"

"He'd be amazing, Sir," Patil said, a sad smile appearing on her face. "You should see him with my two year old cousin. She absolutely worships him, and he plays with her, makes her laugh, sorts her out when she's having a tantrum."

"So if he'd be that amazing, why don't you want to start a family with him?"

"I do," Patil replied quietly. "There's nothing I'd

want more. I mean, he wasn't talking about right now, we'd have to get married first, but, I do really want that with him. But I don't know if I can."

Blake stared at her confused. "Why not?"

Patil clutched the tissue in her hands and glanced at him, looking uncomfortable. "It's a bit of a delicate issue, Sir."

"It won't go any further." Blake told her.

Again, Patil sighed. "I've not even told Matti. That's sort of why we're not great at the minute. I couldn't bring myself to be honest with him. I've got something wrong with me."

Blake's heart skipped a beat. "What?"

Patil must have seen the horrified look in Blake's eye, because she smiled at him again. "It's nothing like that, don't worry. But I don't know if I can have children. I've got PCOS."

For a second, Blake frowned, trying to remember if he had heard the term before, but Patil answered his question for him.

"Polycystic ovary syndrome, Sir. You don't need to know all the ins and outs of it, but it's something I picked up genetically. My mum had it."

"Okay," Blake said. "So, does that mean you can't have children?"

"Not exactly," Patil said, wiping her eyes with the remains of the tissue. "But it can make fertility a lot harder and even if I do get pregnant, there's no guarantee…" Her voice drifted off.

Blake exhaled. "Mini, you need to *tell* him."

"I *know*," Patil exclaimed, starting to cry again. "But I know how much it means to him. He said to me he's always wanted to start a family. What if I can't give him that? I don't want to lose him!" She started sobbing into her tissue again. "And last night, we had another row, because he just thinks I don't want to have kids with him, and I was an idiot. I said he was too immature and then I stormed out. He walked in on me being chatted up by someone. I swear, I wasn't interested, but it's just made things ten times worse."

The door to the meeting room opened and Inspector Royale walked in. "Ah, Blake," he boomed. "Good to see you here early."

Patil quickly rubbed her eyes. "Morning, Sir."

Royale raised his eyebrows. "*Oh*! Mini! Glad to see you're committed. Are you alright to take today's meeting, Blake? I don't feel a hundred percent. I had a bit of a funny turn last night. I'm sure it's just a bug or something, but my wife is insisting I take it easy. Not really possible with this murder to solve, but you know how it is. I'll be in my office if you need anything."

"Right, Sir," Blake said. They watched Royale stroll into the office and close the door behind him.

"Bless him. I could be sat here on fire and he wouldn't notice." Patil smiled.

Before they could say anything else, the door

opened and Gardiner strolled in, soon followed by Mattison and a few other officers.

Blake took one last look at Patil to see if she was alright then stood at the front of the room.

"Good morning, everybody," he began. "Let's get started."

"Have we managed to work out how the killer snuck past you yet?" Gardiner drawled. "Seems to me once we worked that out, it should become a lot easier."

Blake glared at him. He was in no humour for Gardiner's acerbic observations, especially when they were about how the murder had happened right under his nose. "Not as yet, Michael, no. But I'd be delighted to hear any suggestions you have?"

Gardiner shrugged. "Seems to be the only logical way she could possibly have been killed is before you heard that crash. If, as you claim, Thomas Frost has been puppeteering some of his cronies on the outside to do his bidding, it's hardly beyond all reasonable doubt that they could mastermind some sort of elaborate plot."

Blake scratched the back of his head, a deadpan expression on his face. "Such as?"

"How should I know?" Gardiner scoffed. "I'm not a criminal mastermind."

"No, I think we're all fully aware of that, Michael," Blake replied sardonically as he pulled the whiteboard to reveal the case details and photographs. "But you and Inspector Royale were at the flat yesterday. Did you find anything that might be of any help?"

"Yes, I was there," Gardiner drawled, pulling out his notepad. "Fine job for a sergeant, I must say. Trawling through a dead woman's flat."

Mattison groaned loudly. "Did you find anything, yes or no?"

The room went silent for a few moments. Gardiner's eyes bulged. "Don't you speak to *me* like that, Mattison! May I remind you that I am your superior, –"

"That's *enough*," Blake said sharply, eying Mattison pointedly. "Can we get on? What, if anything, did you find at the flat?"

Gardiner flicked through his notebook, flipping the pages with an air of great irritation. "Nothing that we could find relating to how the murder was committed, no. Aside from that leaflet from the clinic, the only thing we found that wasn't in her case notes was a packet of medication in the bathroom. Other than that, no unusual fingerprints, signs of a struggle, or anything."

Blake sighed and rubbed his eyes. "What was the medication?"

Gardiner snorted. "I could hardly pronounce it. Car-bam-aze-pine or something like that."

Blake pulled his phone out of his pocket and pulled up the search engine. "Say it to me again?"

"Car-bam-aze-pine."

After a couple of attempts at spelling what Gardiner had said correctly, Blake finally was presented with what the medication was.

"Not especially helpful," he said, scribbling it into the case file.

"What is it?" Patil asked.

"Epilepsy medication," Blake replied. He stared at the white board again and murmured to himself. "A fact that adds nothing as far as I can see to how a woman could be throttled in a locked apartment, who stuck that note on my door, or why, or how any of it is connected to a serial killer in a prison over thirty miles away." After a few moments of thinking, Blake turned to the room again. "Who have we got in terms of suspects?"

"Apart from your friend in the prison, not a lot," Gardiner replied. "Apart from Jamie Salford," Mattison added. He threw a dirty look at Patil. "And God, do I hope that he did it."

Blake raised a disdainful eyebrow. "Why?"

Mattison glanced at Patil again then looked down at his notes. "I just don't like him."

"We can hardly arrest people for murder just because we don't like them Matti," Blake replied. "Otherwise, the prisons would be ten times more crowded than they already are. What do we have on Salford though?"

Patil cleared her throat. "He's got a criminal record. Nothing concrete to tie him to the murder, though he has got previous for drunken violence."

"And was heard making threats towards Kerry just a few hours before she was killed," Mattison pointed out. "*And* I wouldn't say drunken violence isn't linked to the murder considering when he made those threats, he was, according to a witness, very drunk. It must have been him."

"It's circumstantial, though, Matti," Blake said, sighing. "Yes, in terms of anything else we've got, he is top of the list, but how? Kerry was alive and well when she closed the door of her apartment at about two o'clock, but was dead when we ran inside after we heard that crash."

"Then we bring him in and get him to tell us," Mattison said, throwing his pen down onto the desk.

"You're obsessed, Billy!" Patil exclaimed. "We can't just pull him in without any hard evidence."

Mattison shook his head and savagely opened his notepad again. "That's right, stick up for your boyfriend."

Blake held his hand up. "Can we stop?"

"He's not my boyfriend!" Patil cried shrilly.

"Didn't look that way last night."

"Do we have to do this now? Will you just *grow*

up?"

"So you keep saying!" Mattison shouted back, now ignoring any pretence of trying to keep their argument quiet.

"*Oi*!" Blake shouted. "The pair of you, I want in Inspector Royale's office –"

He was interrupted by Mandy Darnwood walking into the room. "Everyone? Just had a call from Clackton. Somebody called Sonia Carmichael?"

Blake turned to her, frowning. "Sonia? What's happened?"

"She sounded really distressed," Darnwood replied, her bored tone sounding as far away from urgent as it was possible to be. "She says she's found a body of someone she knows. Something about a Jamie Salford?"

The team exchanged glances.

"A body?" Blake repeated, stunned.

"I've got the address," Mandy said, carelessly passing him a post-it note that she had scribbled on. Blake took it from her.

"This is Jamie Salford's address. Alright, everyone with me."

CHAPTER FOURTEEN

Blake looked down at the body on the ground, a mixture of sadness and confusion swimming around his head. The rest of the team gathered round him, Patil in the next room taking a statement from an extremely distressed Sonia.

"Who is he?" Gardiner asked, as they watched Sharon Donahue examine the body.

"His name is Marcus," Blake murmured. "Marcus Langton. He was Jamie Salford's housemate."

"We only spoke to him yesterday," Mattison said.

"Look at the state of his face, Sir. Only Salford could have done this."

"Let's wait till we know all the facts, Matti," Blake told him.

As if on cue, Sharon stood up and addressed them. "Okay, as you can tell by the bruising all around the face, he was given a pretty nasty beating. I would estimate that he was knocked unconscious by a punch in the wrong place."

"Is that what killed him?" Blake asked.

Sharon pulled a face. "No, I don't think so." She knelt down to the body and gently lifted his head. "If you look here, we can see he's been knocked quite hard on the head. Judging by the position, I'd say it was from behind. I'd guess whoever was attacking him just grabbed the nearest thing they could get their hands on."

Blake stared at the battered face of Marcus. "He gets two rounds of hell beaten out of him and then gets whacked on the head?"

Sharon shrugged. "I'd need to examine him further, but a whack this hard, I would say at this point that this is the cause of death."

Blake sighed. "Okay. Thanks, Sharon."

He walked into the living room where he found Patil and Sonia. Sonia was shaking and crying, with Patil gripping tightly onto her hand. They both looked up as Blake entered.

"I'm starting to make a habit of this," Sonia said to him, tears in her eyes.

"What happened, Sonia?" Blake asked her softly.

Sonia shook her head. "It's all a bit of a blur to be honest. I knew Jamie was angry, but I didn't think he was capable of doing something like this."

"What was he angry about?"

"He found out last night that Marcus and Kerry had been seeing each other. In fact, he reckons that Marcus is – *was* – the father of Kerry's baby. There's footage on the apartment security cameras of them together." She took a few deep breaths to calm herself.

"Take your time," Blake told her.

"He turned up last night and found the footage, I don't know how he found out, but he stormed out, threatening about what he was going to do. When I finished work, I came here. I didn't know what he was going to do, I've seen such a dark and dangerous side to him these past couple of weeks. When I got here, Marcus was –" She stopped to stifle another sob. "Marcus was just arriving home. He'd been on a night out, and was only just getting home. I warned him that Jamie knew about Kerry, but then Marcus opened the door and Jamie was just on him. Punching him, kicking him, he just had this absolutely crazed look in his eyes. Then he picked up a vase or something from the side and slammed it into his head, pushed me out the way and ran out of the door. I'm *scared,* Blake.

What if he comes after me next?"

"That won't happen, Sonia," Blake told her firmly. "We're going to find him." He turned to Patil. "Mini, can I leave you to deal with things here?"

"Yes, Sir."

Blake stood up and walked back into the hallway, where he found Mattison writing in his notepad, watching Sharon take Marcus' body away.

"You want to help me find him?" Blake asked him.

Mattison looked up from his notepad. "Too right I do."

"Come on then."

Soon, Blake and Mattison were driving around Clackton, their eyes searching every street and alleyway. Deep down, Blake was not expecting to find him.

"If he's got any sense, he'll still be running as fast as he can," Mattison said as they drove through the centre of town. "He could be miles away by now."

They had already put a call out for surveillance around the town to get in contact with them if they saw anybody fitting Jamie's description, but Blake did not have high hopes.

"While I've got you on your own," Blake said as they scanned the streets around them. "Do you want to tell me what the hell this morning was all about?"

Mattison scratched the back of his head. "It's

nothing, Sir."

"Didn't seem like nothing. Let me save you the effort of trying to fob me off with something, Matti. I've spoken to Mini, I know what this is about."

Mattison turned to him. "You do?"

"Yep. And trust me, it's not what you think. I'm not going to get involved, but let me assure you of one thing. That girl loves you. No accounting for taste, right?"

Mattison rolled his eyes at Blake's joke but smiled, returning his eyes to the street. "Salford was trying to chat her up last night. He was practically all over her. Then when I stopped him, he was all mouth. I just sort of lost it."

"If you think she's got eyes for anyone other than you, then you're more of a dipstick then I thought," Blake told him lightly as he turned the steering wheel in the direction of the train station. "Just talk to her. She's got things she needs to say to you and you need to listen and be there for her."

"Is it anything I've done? Is she alright?" Mattison said quickly, looking worried.

"No and yes, she's fine," Blake reassured him. "Just promise me, you'll show her how much you love her."

Mattison nodded. "I do, I just think that – *there!*"

Blake's eyes shot to where Mattison was pointing. Across the road from the train station was Jamie

Salford. He had a hood up and was clearly doing his best to look inconspicuous, but it was definitely him. He walked quickly down the street towards them, but had not yet seen them.

"Right," Blake said, quickly unbuckling his seatbelt. "Let's go."

They got out of the car and began walking towards Jamie. The traffic was busy on the roads around them, giving Blake hope that if he did try and make a run for it, he was limited in where he could go.

Then, he looked up and spotted them. For a few moments, he did not move, clearly weighing up his options. But then, in the blink of an eye, Jamie turned on his feet and ran in the opposite direction.

There were two roads to cross between them and the traffic was heavy. As Blake and Mattison sprinted towards the fleeing Jamie, they held up their ID cards and shouted "*Police!*" in the hope that the drivers of the car would notice and allow them to cross.

All the time, Blake kept Jamie in his sights, but he was a lot faster than he looked. In front of him was another busy road, but the cars were slowing to stop at a traffic light. He danced between them, and hopped over a barrier, almost getting hit by a lorry as he ran into the path of oncoming traffic in the opposite lane.

All the while, Blake and Mattison were getting closer. But as Blake looked to where Jamie was headed, his heart sank. He was running straight towards the train station.

As they pursued him, Blake hurriedly called for backup into his radio, though he was unsure if there was any point if Jamie managed to get on a train.

They ran into the station forecourt, just as Jamie disappeared through the entrance.

"There's a train on the platform ahead, Sir!" Mattison cried.

Clackton station was in the middle of the main line, meaning that fast trains often passed through it, and trains that did stop here quickly picked up speed once they were underway.

As they ran into the station, they saw Jamie glance over his shoulder and sprint towards the platform. There were people bustling everywhere, alighting from the train that had stopped and briefly Blake lost sight of him. But then, they saw him again as he vaulted over the ticket barrier. The security standing by shouted out to him and tried to stop him, but he was too quick for them.

Through the gaps in the crowd, they saw Jamie dive into the train, just as the doors were closing. Blake cursed loudly as they pushed their way through the crowd, holding their IDs up at the security team and yelling to be let through the gate.

Finally, they reached the platform, but the train was now moving.

"*Stop the train!*" Blake yelled, with Mattison in

close pursuit.

The guard on the platform realised what was happening and ran after them along the platform, blowing his whistle frantically to try and attract the driver's attention, but it was too late. At the end of the platform was a large fence. As the last carriage clattered past Blake, he reached the fence and kicked it.

But, as he turned to Mattison so they could find out where the train was going, and try and get it stopped at its next station, a blur ran past him.

"Matti!" shouted Blake.

Mattison could apparently not hear him. He had vaulted himself over the fence and was now sprinting as fast as he could alongside the track, to catch up to the train.

CHAPTER
FIFTEEN

Panting wildly as his heart thumped in his chest, Jamie sank into his seat, trying to catch his breath. He could not believe how much trouble he was in, and the suspicious looks of his fellow passengers were not helping his paranoia either. He was trying to work out what his next move should be. Whatever the next stop was, he decided, he would get off there, try and avoid any police, and lie low until they hopefully forgot about him.

His knuckles were still throbbing from where he

had punched Marcus, so he wrung his hands together to massage them and looked out the window. What he saw made him forget about the pain in his knuckles. Mattison running towards him, alongside the track, his legs almost a blur to keep up with the train.

The passengers started murmuring around him as they spotted the policeman, wondering what was going on. The train was starting to pick up speed, but Mattison just ran faster. For a moment, their eyes met. Jamie's wide in horror, Mattison's narrowed in fury and determination. He pulled out his ID card and held it up the air, screaming at the top of his lungs for the train to stop.

"*Oh*! It's a policeman, Mildred!" an old man in the next seat to him said. "I think he wants us to stop."

"Should I press the emergency button?" Mildred asked him, watching Mattison with interest.

"*No!*" Jamie yelled.

It was the worst thing he could have done.

"He's after *that* guy," another voice said. "*Quick*! Press the button."

"I'm not getting a fine! *You* do it!"

"It's only a fine if it's not an emergency, quick!"

"*Don't!*" yelled Jamie, but it was too late. The train jerked forward, the brakes screeching. Jamie put his head in his hands.

As the train finally ground to a halt, it did not take long for Mattison to attract the driver's attention. The doors shuddered open. The passengers pointed Mattison in direction of Jamie's seat. Mattison yanked him up and cuffed him. Jamie saw Blake pull himself up to the train, followed by a few other police officers.

"You are *very* under arrest," Mattison said to him, but changed his tone when he saw Blake.

"Jamie Salford, I'm arresting you for the murders of Marcus Langton and Kerry Nightingale," he said loudly, frogmarching him along the corridor of the train as the passengers clapped around him.

The interview room in Harmschapel police station was cold and draughty, and now he was sat here, alone, and now able to comprehend what lay ahead of him, Jamie was scared. He had been arrested for two murders, neither of which he knew whether he had committed or not. He could not see any way out of his current situation.

The door opened and Blake strolled in. Behind him, Mattison also appeared and sat down.

"I don't want *him* in here," Jamie snapped.

Blake glanced at Mattison. "Why not? Because he arrested you?"

"He was going to punch me in the bar the other night. His girlfriend had to hold him back. I don't feel safe with him here."

Blake raised an eyebrow. "There's only one person in his room with knuckles that make you look like you've done a few rounds with Mike Tyson, Jamie." He pressed the record button on the machine.

"Interview commencing at eleven thirty five AM. Present in the room are Detective Sergeant Blake Harte, Police Constable Billy Mattison, and Jamie Salford." He paused and looked up at Jamie.

"You're getting nothing out of me," Jamie snapped, glaring at Mattison.

"I'd like to start with your housemate, Marcus," Blake said, ignoring him. "How long you lived with him?"

"No comment," Jamie replied. He had seen this sort of procedure on enough television shows to know it was the only hope he had whilst he tried and thought of some sort of alibi for himself.

"Have you known him long?"

"No comment."

"What happened to your knuckles, Jamie?"

"No comment."

"Did you get in a fight?"

"No comment."

"A fight because you found out that Marcus had been seeing Kerry behind your back?"

Jamie glared at him, the fury from the revelation rearing its head again.

"*No comment,*" he said, through gritted teeth.

Blake rolled his eyes, an action that annoyed Jamie further. "See, the whole *'no comment'* routine only really works when we *don't* have any evidence, Jamie. And, unfortunately for you, we do. We *know* that Marcus was in a secret relationship with Kerry, we *know* that you confronted him, we *know* you battered the life out of him, and then whacked him in the back of the head with a vase for good measure, and we *know* that –"

Jamie's head shot to him, frowning. "What?"

Blake stopped mid-sentence. "Sorry?"

"What are you on about? Whacked him round the head with a vase?"

Blake glanced at Mattison. "The vase that is in your house, of which we found fragments embedded in his skull, Jamie. The vase that you used to kill Marcus after you had finished giving him a beating."

"I didn't use a vase? All I did was beat him up. It's *true! D*on't pull that face at me," he snapped, pointing at Mattison who had raised his eyebrows in disdain.

"Well, why don't you tell us what *did* happen?" Blake suggested, holding his arms out.

Jamie sipped from the plastic cup of water on the table and shrugged. If he could convince them that he genuinely had no idea what they were talking about with the vase, maybe he could prove that he had had nothing to do with Kerry's death either.

"Come on, Jamie," Blake continued. "Two people you cared about are dead. If it wasn't you that was responsible, don't you want to help us find out who is?"

Jamie hesitated, then nodded. "Marcus wasn't home when I got back last night, he was on one of his benders, probably out pulling some other bloke's bird."

He and Mattison exchanged looks.

"Go on," Blake urged.

"So, I had all night to sit and think about it. All that did was make me angrier, cause I realised how many lies he must have told me. All the times he listened to me upset after she dumped me, and it was because of him the *entire* time!"

"Did he tell you that?"

Jamie nodded. "When he finally got back the next morning, I confronted him about it. Not gonna lie, I was really mad. He started giving me all this crap about how I was too intense for her, she just wanted a fling before she went to Spain, and how he was so perfect for her. Then I asked him about the baby, and he didn't even have the nerve to look me in the eye. He just looked down at the floor and mumbled about how sorry he was." He looked up at the ceiling, remembering the emotions he had been feeling at the time and shrugged. "Then I just lost it.

"Sonia came round then, panicking about what I was gonna do to Marcus, but obviously I'd already done it. He was in a pretty big mess by the time she got there. I'd just seen red and let my fists do the talking. I've been trying to get a control over my anger, but nothing seems to be working." He looked up at Blake, hoping that what he was saying would act as some form of defence. "I've not had what most people have had. Y'know, a loving upbringing, people to comfort me. I had Kerry, and I had Marcus. But even *they* stabbed me in the back. I *loved* that woman. I'd have done anything for her. But she just didn't care. Anything she wanted, I'd have done it for her. Even going to some of her really boring restaurants, 'cause she couldn't go in any of the bars because of the lights."

Blake was frowning at him, as if something was not making sense to him. "What happened when Sonia arrived?"

Jamie shuffled in his seat. "She walked in and Marcus was on the floor. To be honest, yeah, I thought I'd killed him. He was breathing I think, but he wasn't moving. She started going on about how I was already up to my neck in it because of Kerry, how it was obvious that I had killed Marcus, and that I better get running."

Blake leant forwards across the table. "And what about Thomas Frost?"

Jamie frowned. "Who?"

"Thomas Frost. Does the name Thomas Frost mean anything to you at all?"

Jamie shook his head, confused. "No?"

"Interview suspended at eleven forty-one AM." Blake stood up. "Matti, charge him for assault, and put him in the cell."

Mattison looked confused and followed Blake out of the room. "*Sir?*"

Jamie watched them both leave, only vaguely curious by the change of questioning. Whatever happened from this point onwards, he knew his life was going to have to change.

CHAPTER
SIXTEEN

Blake walked out of the interview room, and leant against the wall. Mattison stared at him, looking completely clueless.

"*Sir?*" he said. "What's going on? I thought we had him?"

"Matti, he doesn't know anything about the vase used to kill Marcus. Or anything about Thomas Frost."

"He's *lying*! He *knows* we've got him!"

"Exactly. He was running from us, then we caught him. What's the point in lying at this stage? We could pin absolutely any of this on him, he's got motive, means, and the temperament. And he knows that. Why the hell would he lie?" Blake turned on his heels and strolled towards the exit. "Like I said, charge him and put him in the cells for assault. Leave him there till I get back."

"Where are you going?"

But Blake was already gone.

"Right, thanks, Sally. I can't say I'm surprised. Frost has been clever, I'll give him that."

Blake was sat in his car, outside Clayton Apartments, looking up at the top flat.

"Blake, if you manage to prove that's how it was done, then you deserve a promotion," Sally told him. "Good luck."

"Thanks," Blake murmured. "I'm going to need it."

He hung up the phone and got out the car. With one last look at the top of the building where Kerry's balcony could just be seen protruding from the top, he knocked on the glass door. Sonia poked her head over the reception desk, then pressed the release button under her desk to allow him to enter.

"Blake? Everything okay?"

"Hi, Sonia. I'm surprised to see you working, after what happened."

"I wanted to keep busy," Sonia replied, shrugging

as she placed her book down on the desk. "Besides, with everything that's happening with Jamie, there's spare shifts, and who am I to turn down money?"

Blake nodded. "There were just a couple more things I needed to check over in Kerry's flat. Would you mind letting me in?"

"Sure thing," Sonia said, heaving her huge frame out of the chair. "Has Jamie been charged?"

"I can't discuss that, sorry," Blake said, smiling. "You should know that, being such a fan of crime."

"True," Sonia said as they entered the lift. The musty and dirty smell she always exuded smelt worse in the confined lift.

When they arrived at the top floor, Sonia reached to her belt and produced her lanyard, stretching the elastic so that the key reached the keyhole. "Help yourself," she said, opening the door.

"You can come in with me, if you like," Blake said. "There was just something I wanted to check in the bedroom."

Sonia nodded and followed him into the apartment. Everything was much the same as it had been when Blake had last been here. He walked straight to the bedroom and pressed the light switch. Nothing happened. The room stayed dark.

"Oh, is the light gone again?" Blake asked.

"Yeah," Sonia said, rolling her eyes. "I told you they were useless."

Blake stood on the bed and pulled down the lampshade. "Do you know what, Sonia? I think I might have solved the light bulb problem in this place. In this apartment, anyway." He held up the light fitting so that she could see it. "I always find that it helps if there's a bulb inserted for there to be light. Mind you, what do I know? I'm no technician."

Sonia did not reply. Blake continued examining the bulb less light fitting. "When did you first get in contact with Thomas Frost?" he asked her casually.

Sonia's face dropped. "What do you mean?"

Blake stepped down off the bed. "Thomas Frost. The man who you masterminded this whole thing with? Actually, that's not giving you anywhere near enough credit, because Frost had absolutely no part in Marcus' death, did he?"

Sonia was slowly backing away from, looking slightly horrified, sweat glistening on her brow. "What are you talking about? I have *no* idea what you're on about."

"All the crime books I always see you with. I can't understand why I never twigged. You're *obsessed* with crime. You know all about it. I'm going to hazard a guess at a scenario, Sonia. I think you followed the case of Thomas Frost carefully, all his murders, everything he did, right down to the prison he was incarcerated in. Then, you started writing to him, telling him how much you admired him, respected him, and wanted to start some form of relationship with him."

"You've got *quite* the imagination, I'll give you that," Sonia said, looking less convincing by the second.

"And he reeled you in, because that's how Frost works," Blake said, sighing. "He sees a weakness and he prays on it. You could not have come along at a better time. Frost was watching Kerry's career as a politician bloom, and she was always the one that got away. But of course, you knew that. Being such a devoted fan girl."

Sonia's eyes widened. "I know his work, yeah, but –"

"Sorry?" Blake laughed. "His *work?* He's an evil serial killer, Sonia. If the circumstances had been different, you could have been just another one of his victims!"

"He would *never* do that to *me*!" Sonia snapped, her hand shooting to her mouth before she had even finished the sentence.

Blake shook his head. He almost felt sorry for her, but pity was probably more accurate. "He used you, Sonia. He's without compassion, without empathy. You were just a pawn to him. I read some of the letters he gets. Do you know how many women write to him every week? You're not the first, and you sure as hell won't be the last. But you were the easiest. He sensed your loneliness and your vulnerability, and used you.

You lived close to Kerry, and as the months went by, he turned you into his own personal little assassin, didn't he?"

"He told me he loved me," Sonia murmured, tears forming in her eyes. "He said we could be together."

"When did he say that?"

"When I visited him," Sonia mumbled.

Blake nodded. "According to his prison visitor file, the only person who's been to see Thomas Frost in the past few years has been his son, Simon. Except, as it turns out, Simon Frost now lives abroad. He moved to Australia only a year after his father went to prison. He lives Down Under with a new life. So, who was going to visit him in his son's place?"

Sonia threw herself down on the sofa with her head in her hands. "He got me in touch with some of his contacts," she said quietly. "They got me a false ID card so I could masquerade as his relative. I applied for a visiting order, told them that there had been a typo on their system and that Thomas didn't have a son called Simon, he had a daughter called Simone. Just one letter out. It seemed like such a harmless thing to do so we could meet and be together." She sighed and smiled, staring out in front of her. "That first time we saw each other was everything I hoped it would be and more. I just wish I'd been able to touch him. We couldn't obviously, because of the glass."

Blake walked across the room and sat next to her

on the sofa. "And then he worked his magic on you, and convinced you that Kerry had to die."

Sonia looked at Blake, a sliver of shame on her face. "I did like Kerry, but you said yourself how in love you are with your partner. You'd kill for him, that's *exactly* what you said."

Blake had never regretted his own words more. "Jamie was just perfect for you, wasn't he? And he knows absolutely nothing about Thomas Frost, but I bet Frost knows all about him, right? The pair of you planned this to the letter. But it was a sick plan, Sonia. I don't think I've ever seen a murder so callous as the one you committed when you killed Kerry."

He stood up and looked into the bedroom again. "A whole room where you could hide a murder weapon. And forensics searched from top to bottom, believe me. But why on earth would they look in the lampshade? Because that crash that we heard wasn't Kerry being killed was it?"

Sonia looked down at the floor, a tear rolling down her cheek.

"It was Kerry collapsing. I would never have worked it out, until Jamie mentioned that Kerry couldn't go to the same bars as him because of the lights. There are different forms of epilepsy, but what only a few people seemed to know was that Kerry suffered from photosensitive epilepsy. And you used *that* to kill her."

Sonia put her head in her hands. "It meant that she couldn't know what I was doing to her. I don't think I could have gone through with it if she'd been fully aware."

"You mentioned that you used to be a technician at one of the bars in town," Blake continued, looking at her with disgust and disbelief. "So you know how to set up disco lights and how to alter the intensity of the bulb. When you changed the light bulb in her bedroom that night, you didn't use one of Clayton Apartment's bulbs that infamously never worked. You used one you'd made yourself. One you'd be able to activate and control from outside the flat. I'm guessing on one of those small remote control things that you get for fibrotic lights?

"You knew she was waking up at eight. Us hearing the alarm through the door was your cue. You gave me some rubbish about her using the shower so that I'd be far enough away to give you just enough time to do what you needed to do. Once the alarm had gone off, you activated the bulb. The flashing and intensity of it was so severe that she must have collapsed and start fitting straight away, hence the crash we heard. Once we ran inside, idiot that I am, I let you persuade me to check in the bathroom first which gave you enough time to run in the bedroom and strangle her, made a lot easier by the fact that she was incapacitated, and the last thing you're supposed to do with someone having a seizure or a fit is restrict them. It's on any first aid course. Then you switched the light off just as I ran in and as far as I'm concerned she had been strangled by some phantom that was able to get in before either of us had got there.

"And of course your murder weapon disappeared as soon as you'd let go of it. Straight back onto your waist. A long piece of elastic that keeps the keys to the apartment attached to you at all times. I walk in and you release it from round her neck. One throttled victim, and not a murder weapon to be seen."

Sonia remained silent for a few moments, then she looked up at Blake and gave him a small smile. "Thomas said you were clever. I think you were half the reason why he wanted to do all this. To get one over on the man who locked him up."

"Which would explain why you felt the need to post that poster on my door after you'd followed me home," Blake added. "The speed you drove back here before I could reach must have been amazing, so much so that you ran a guy off the road. Still, what did other people's lives matter so long as you kept yourself out of the limelight? Jamie couldn't have been more useful to you if he had been under Frost's control himself, with him going around threatening Kerry and beating Marcus black and blue. All you had to do to make him look doubly capable of killing Kerry was to just whack Marcus hard enough to finish him off. The finger of blame would then go directly to Jamie."

As Blake put the handcuffs on her wrists and read her rights, Sonia looked around the apartment, apparently trying to take in the normal surroundings around her before she was taken away.

"Just one question you never answered, Blake," she said, looking up at him.

"What's that?"

"Do you think I'll ever find love? True love?"

Blake looked down at her in pity and led her down the corridor. "Who knows, Sonia? Maybe one day someone will write to you."

CHAPTER
SEVENTEEN

When Blake arrived back at the station, Sonia was put in a cell, though he made sure it was one as far away from Jamie as possible. He walked into the meeting room where the rest of the team were waiting for him.

"So, we weren't kidding when we said it happened right under your nose?" Gardiner called pompously.

Blake ignored him, instead turning to Patil and Mattison. "How are you two?"

They looked at each other, cautiously but happily.

"We're good, Sir." Patil said. "We're going to have a long chat tonight about the future."

"But, we're in a good place," Mattison added, before glancing at Patil. "Aren't we?"

She nodded and kissed him on the cheek.

At that moment, Inspector Royale entered the room. He looked distracted, and a little confused.

"You alright, Sir?" Blake asked him.

Royale turned to him, a slightly vacant expression on his face. "Hmm? Yes, yes. Well done. I've just got a bit of a headache, that's all. I'll join you in a minute."

Blake watched him walk unsteadily into his office and was just about to follow him in when Mandy Darnwood poked her head round the door. "DS Harte? You have a visitor."

Blake smiled happily as Harrison entered. "Sorry if I'm interrupting," he said, waving at the others.

"Not at all, in fact, I could not be happier to see you," Blake said, wrapping his arms around him. "How goes the moving in?"

"Oh, *congratulations!*" Patil said. "You never said, Sir!"

"Work and relationships don't mix, Mini. Present company excluded of course."

"It's going alright," Harrison said. "I didn't know whether you were finished or not, I thought we could have some dinner out?"

"Sounds good to me," Blake said. "We need to

have a long conversation too. Except ours concerns goats. And sheds. And huge padlocks."

There was a little ripple of laughter around the room as Harrison looked up at Blake in mock outrage.

"I'll just finish up here," Blake told Harrison. "Let me just give these documents to the Inspector and I should be right with you."

He picked up the papers from his desk and strolled towards Royale's office, knocking on the door as he entered. Royale's chair was spun round and facing the window. "Sir, can you check these through?" Blake asked him. "I need to just –" But immediately Blake knew something was wrong. He threw the documents down on the desk and spun the chair round. "Sir?"

The sight awaiting him made him recoil in horror. Royale's face had dropped on one side, his eyes closed. His body appeared limp and lifeless. He had had a stroke.

"Call an ambulance!" Blake yelled into the meeting room. As pandemonium broke out, Blake checked to see if Royale was breathing and whether there was a pulse. He could feel nothing. Moving him onto the floor, he immediately began CPR as he heard Darnwood on the phone behind him.

But by the time the paramedics had arrived, there was still no response from Royale. Though they wheeled him out on the stretcher, performing the chest pumps all the way, Blake could sense it was too late.

They followed the paramedics to the door and watched as Royale was quickly loaded into the ambulance and was driven away. The siren wailed loudly, echoing around the village, the residents of which who were soon to discover that their numbers had been lessened by one.

ONE WEEK LATER

The funeral was the most beautiful Blake could remember. He had only been to one other funeral for a policeman, which had also been a great occasion, but the camaraderie amongst the people of Harmschapel had moved him so much that by the time the huge procession, which seemed to contain almost everybody in the village, had been led out of St Abra's church, Blake had been in tears.

Harrison gripped Blake's hand as they all walked back to the station together. "That was a really nice speech you made in there. I'm proud of you."

Blake had been called upon to give a eulogy for Royale on behalf of the station and had taken the time to point out all his attributes that had made him such as delight to work under. Blake's life had greatly improved since moving to Harmschapel and he had always partly held Royale in acclaim for that. He just wished he had had the chance to say it.

"I can't believe he's gone," Patil said, dabbing her eyes with a tissue. "What happens at the station now?"

"What do you mean?" Blake asked.

"Will you be promoted, Sir?" Mattison asked, linking arms with Patil. "Seems like the obvious thing to do, what with you being second in command."

"It doesn't quite work like that, Mattison," boomed Gardiner. "They'll need to do internal interviews. Make sure they speak to *all* the people that would be right for the job." He adjusted his tie, causing Mattison to laugh out loud.

"*You?* You think they'll make *you* Inspector of the station?"

"Hey, Matti," Blake said, tapping him on the arm. "There's no reason why Michael could not make Inspector. No reason at all." He exchanged a meaningful look with Harrison, implying that the day Gardiner was put in charge of the station was the day he would resign.

As they arrived at the station, Harrison kissed Blake goodbye and walked home. He had now officially moved in and the only thing left to do was to complete the shed for Betty. Blake had a quietly optimistic feeling that she was even starting to get used to him, by which she had not tried to head butt him for the last two days.

When they entered the station, they found Darnwood stood at the desk looking pensive. "How was the service?" she asked delicately.

"Beautiful," Blake replied. "We sent the old boy out in style."

There was a murmuring of agreement around the other officers.

"Good," Darnwood said, glancing at the meeting room. "We've got a visitor."

They all exchanged glances and hurried to the meeting room. It appeared empty, but as they all walked in, a man appeared in the doorway of Royale's office. He was very tall, almost skeletal looking, with silver stemmed spectacles on the edge of his thin nose. If Blake had not have known better, he would have confused the man for a ballet dancer, but the uniform he was wearing left no mistake as to who this stranger was to be.

"Ah," he said sharply as they all gathered. "Glad you could all make it."

"We've been to a funeral," Blake replied, eyeing him cautiously. "May I ask who you are?"

The man picked up an inspector's hat from the

desk and placed it smartly on top of his head. "Angel. Inspector Jacob Angel. I shall be taking over from Inspector Royale after his sad passing." The man could not have sounded less grieved if he had tried. "I assume you're all back on duty now? Carry on. Detective Sergeant Harte, is it?"

Blake stared at him, agog. Already, the apparent difference between Royale and Angel's personas were staggering. "Yes?"

"Yes, *Sir,*" Angel corrected. "Don't let *that* happen again, incidentally, but I'd like to see you in my office when you have a moment." He held the office door open, apparently to indicate that the '*moment*' was to be immediately.

Blake and the other officers all exchanged horrified looks. It seemed things in Harmschapel station were about to change.

REACH

To keep up to date with **Robert Innes'** future releases, follow him on **Facebook** at:

facebook.com/RobertInnesAuthor

Printed in Great Britain
by Amazon